KEIKO'S WAR

BY

JOHN C. DALGLISH

2017

DECEMBER 7, 1941

December 7, 1941 broke as a warm, sunny day in the San Francisco Bay area. Jesse Sommers and his mother Estelle attended church services with Uncle Jerry and Aunt Carol. As usual, the church was crowded with families. It was nearing noon and they were singing the final hymn, when the doors at the back of the church swung open with a crash.

Someone came running down the center aisle, yelling incoherently. The music abruptly stopped.

"Pearl has been attacked!"

Jesse turned toward the commotion, and spotted a young man standing at the podium, looking back at the congregation. His face was beaded with sweat and his eyes were flared wide with fear.

Father Malone approached the man. "I'm sorry, son, what did you say?"

"The Japs bombed Pearl Harbor this morning!"

The crowd seemed to freeze—only the rapid breathing of the young man breaking the silence.

"Are you sure?"

"I'm sure! It's all over the radio."

Each member of the congregation struggled to process the news. A murmur slowly grew inside the sanctuary. Then—as if an invisible dam had broken loose—chaos erupted.

Everyone started yelling and trying to exit the church at once. Fear rolled over the congregation like an ocean wave, and the silence of the minute before, was replaced by an uproar that flowed out into the street.

Jesse looked down at his mother. She was sitting with her hands folded, her lips silently moving in prayer. He did his best to shield her from the commotion around them.

Uncle Jerry and Aunt Carol had been among the first to exit, bolting for a side door before most people had figured out what was going on.

Eventually, Jesse and his mother were left alone with the minister and a few others. Most were praying, some weeping.

He touched her shoulder. "Are you ready to go, Mom?"

She nodded slowly, opened her eyes, and stood. "I was praying for your cousins."

"Blair and Tony?"

"Yes. They're stationed in Hawaii."

It shook him deep inside. Someone he knew was in the middle of the attack.

It was then Keiko flooded into his consciousness.

If the Japanese had attacked America,

nothing for her or her family would ever be the same. He was consumed with one thought.

He had to get to Keiko.

EIGHTEEN MONTHS EARLIER

****

JULY, 1941

"Open the door, Keiko."

"Yes, Father."

She finished tying her long hair into a loose bun in an effort to keep her neck cool. She inserted a white hair that was a bold contrast to her jet-black locks. Early July was always hot in San Francisco, but especially this year, and her long hair seemed like a blanket. She moved to the front door of her parent's small restaurant, flipped the lock open, and raised the blind.

The restaurant was her father's idea after mother got a reputation for her cooking. Azumi Yoshida would bring noodles or soup to community functions, and so many people raved to her father, that he decided to open *Takeshi's*

Japanese Eatery. It was Keiko's opinion the restaurant should bear the name of her mother, but her father insisted he would be humiliated if it were named as such, so he called it after himself.

After renting a small building on the corner of Sutter and Laguna, near the edge of what some called Japanese Peoples Town, he put in some booths and tables, bought the kitchen equipment with a loan from his mother, and opened the doors.

Word spread quickly about the food, and before long, the diner had a regular clientele of both Japanese and non-Japanese patrons. Father served as greeter and seating host, making a point to know the names of every customer. Keiko had been working for her parents here since her sophomore year in high school.

At first, she'd started by helping in the kitchen, mostly fetching ingredients or utensils her mother needed. Now, Keiko served as the seating host, taking over her father's duties when she graduated high school. Still coming to the restaurant every day, he would sit in the back booth holding court, as if he were some ancient emperor.

Keiko disliked her father sitting around while Azumi did all the cooking, but many things about Takeshi Yoshida displeased her.

"Table for one, please."

Keiko looked up, startled by the voice, and

surprised she hadn't heard the door open. The young man standing in front of her was smiling, his blue eyes staring directly into hers, briefly stealing her tongue.

"Ah, sure…of course." She grabbed a menu. "Where would you like to sit? You have your choice."

"Right there would be fine."

Her gaze followed his extended arm to the spot he'd selected—directly behind her station. "Oh, okay. Here's your menu."

Keiko left to get him a glass of water and when she returned, he closed his menu to watch her approach the table. "It's my first time here. What's good?"

She set the water down. "Well, my mother is the cook, and her noodles are the most popular thing on the menu."

"How about her soups, are they good?"

"Oh my, yes! Her miso with seaweed and vegetables is amazing!"

Realizing he was grinning, her outburst caused her to blush.

He handed her the menu. "Miso sounds good."

"Great." She went and put in his order, and when she turned around, several other customers had come in. The lunch rush had begun.

Ninety minutes later, as the lunch crowd waned, she felt a light tap on her shoulder.

"Excuse me."

She turned, finding the blue eyes watching her again. "Yes?"

"I wanted to say you were absolutely correct."

His stare managed to turn her into a high school girl again. She stared without answering.

"The miso? You said it was good."

"Oh…oh, yes. Of course."

"Well, you were right. Please tell your mother that it was the best I've ever tasted."

"I will, and thank you for saying so."

"You're welcome."

He handed her the tab and a couple dollars before leaving. Keiko watched him go, and then went to ring up the total. Scrawled across the bottom of the restaurant ticket was a note.

Wonderful meal. Jesse.

Keiko smiled. "Nice to meet you, Jesse with the blue eyes."

"Who?"

Keiko turned to find her sister Hotaru had arrived from school. Hotaru, which in Japanese means firefly, was the perfect name for her sister. She was constantly in motion and seemed to bring a smile to every face. "Did you see him, Roo?"

"See who?"

"The guy with the blue eyes who was just in here."

Hotaru looked toward the street, then back

at her sister. "You'll have to be more specific."

"Well, he was..." Keiko realized she didn't remember much about the young man except his eyes. "Never mind; I'll point him out if he ever comes in again."

Her younger sister grinned at her. "Wow, my older sister speechless. He must've been cute."

Keiko spotted their father, his gaze locked on them. "Keep it down, Roo. Father is watching."

"Okay, okay. Relax, it's not like you're going to marry him."

"Of course not, but Father will think so!"

Hotaru laughed, and headed back toward the kitchen. "Your secret is safe with me."

"What secret?"

"Exactly...what secret?"

****

A few days later, Keiko was clearing off a table next to the front window, when a shadow passed in front of her. She looked up to see Jesse opening the front door. She quickly finished, took the plates to the kitchen, and hurried to her station. He was smiling at her as she approached, and she returned his grin with one of her own. "Hello, again. Would you like a table?"

"Actually, I would like food."

It took her a second to realize he was joking, but when she did, her face reddened. "Follow me, please."

She picked up a menu and started toward the back of the restaurant. Stopping at a table midway between the kitchen and the front door, she laid the menu down. "I hope this will be…"

She turned to find him still standing by the door, pointing at the booth next to her station.

"I hope you don't mind, I like this table."

"No, not at all."

He refused her offer of a menu. "I won't need that. Water and Miso will be perfect."

"Great. I'll put in your order."

Keiko took a better look at Jesse before retreating to the kitchen. The blue eyes were as she remembered, almost crystalline in their clarity, but he was taller than she recalled. She guessed him to be just under six feet, and while not muscular, a certain strength emanated from him. His light brown hair was neatly fixed, and his clothes were new, but not flashy.

Jesse had come in after the lunch rush this time, and Hotaru was already there working. Keiko stopped next to her sister, filled a glass of water, and tried to speak without moving her lips. "He's here."

"Who's here?"

"The guy with the blue eyes—the one I

told you about."

Hotaru looked up over the serving wall, standing on her toes. "Where?"

Keiko reached over and pulled her sister's arm. "Get down! I don't want him to know we're talking about him."

"Is he the one by your station?"

"Yes."

"He's cute, I guess."

"What do you mean, I guess?"

"I don't know, not my type."

Keiko rolled her eyes. "You're too young to have a *type*!"

Their mother stopped behind them. "What are you two talking about?"

Hotaru started to answer but Keiko cut her off. "Nothing, Mother. Just silly stuff."

"I see. Has anyone taken that young man's order?"

Keiko handed her the ticket. "A bowl of miso."

Azumi stared at the stranger in the booth, then gave her eldest daughter a suspicious look.

Keiko held her breath, but her mother didn't pry. "I'll have the soup up in a minute."

****

The beautiful Japanese girl was standing at her station when Jesse Sommers finished his soup and pushed the bowl to the edge of the table.

"The soup was wonderful again."

She turned to him, maybe a little too quickly. "I'm glad you liked it. You should try the noodles sometime."

"I'll make a point to do that. May I ask your name?"

"Keiko."

His heart fluttered slightly. "That's beautiful."

Her black hair was thick, and judging by the size of the bun, long. Her deep brown eyes entranced him, and seemed like pools of emotion waiting to be released. She appeared delicate, but he sensed an inner strength, a powerful determination, that ebbed below the surface. "I noticed you didn't ask what my name was."

Her eyes averted from his gaze, but returned quickly. "I…I saw your note the last time you were in…Jesse."

It pleased him immensely she remembered his name, and it flowed off her tongue like breeze on a warm afternoon, slowly drifting across the bay. Needing to get back to the office, he stood and gave her a couple dollars. "It was very nice to meet you, Keiko."

She smiled warmly "And you, Jesse."

****

Keiko had not seen her father come in the back door. When she finished ringing up Jesse's check, she picked up his bowl, and headed back to the kitchen.

"Keiko!"

She jumped, almost dropping the bowl. "Yes, Father?"

"May I have a word?"

She set the bowl down on the nearest table and went to her father's booth. "Yes, Father?"

He gestured at the seat across from him. "Sit."

She did, and waited.

His eyes locked with hers. "Who was that boy?"

"What boy?"

His stare was unflinching. "Do not play innocent with me, Daughter."

Heat began to climb her neck and her face reddened, a reaction invariably produced by her father's scrutiny.

"He's a customer, Father. I was just being polite."

"Do I need to remind you of your responsibility to this family?"

"Of course not, Father."

He was silent for several minutes as she did her best to look unconcerned. Finally, he reached for his cup of Saki.

"Be careful your eyes don't lead you where your heart cannot follow, Daughter."

"Yes, Father."

Knowing she'd been dismissed, Keiko stood and went to the kitchen. Hotaru had been watching everything, and rolled her eyes as Keiko passed.

"Father is in a pleasant mood today."

Keiko gave her sister a wry smile. "Isn't he always?"

****

After lunch, Jesse headed back to his office in Buena Vista Park. His Uncle Jerry owned *Sommers Property Management*. After the death of his father, Jesse had joined the company. Though not the future Jesse had hoped for, it accomplished what was most important to Jesse, taking care of his mother.

Enrolled at City College of San Francisco, he was just finishing his freshman year when his father had a stroke. Michael Sommers died two days later, leaving Jesse and his mother Estelle, alone. At the funeral, his uncle had taken Jesse aside.

"Do you have an idea what you and your mother will do now?"

Jesse had shaken his head, still too stunned

to consider even the next day. "Not really."

"You've been to my office. How would you feel about coming to work for me?"

He'd not considered it, and the idea of working in real estate had not appealed to him, but it was obvious he would need to do something. "I don't know. I really hadn't got that far yet."

Uncle Jerry rested a hand on his shoulder.

"I understand, it's all very sudden, but think about it. You know your aunt and I have no kids of our own, and one day I'll need to retire. I'd be glad to have you on board."

Jesse was deeply touched by the offer, and though it wasn't his dream job, it was just a couple days later when he discussed it with his mother.

"Uncle Jerry offered to take me on at his company, Mother."

"I heard. That was very kind of him."

"I know."

Estelle, her green eyes now carrying a sadness her blonde hair could not conceal, touched Jesse's face. "What about college?"

Jesse knew the truth. His parents didn't have any savings, and his mother wouldn't be able to pay the bills alone, never mind help him go to college.

"That can come later. Right now, I'm more concerned about you."

His mother started to weep again, or

maybe she hadn't ever stopped, he wasn't sure. "I love you, Son."

"I love you too, Mother."

Jesse had worked for his uncle ever since and even grown to enjoy the job.

He parked the 1934 Chevrolet Master Sedan he'd inherited from his father outside the office. Jesse was glad to have a vehicle, but the large black box wasn't very sporty for a guy in his early twenties. Still, like his job, it served the purpose.

Inside the office, his uncle was busy with a client. Janet, their receptionist, was on the phone. He sat at his desk and recalled the brown eyes and soft skin of Keiko. She had been fixed in his memory since the first day he'd seen her, and he'd made up his mind that lunch at *Takeshi's* should become a regular stop for him.

"Have you had lunch yet?" His uncle was looking over at him, the client having left.

"Yeah, I stopped at that Japanese place I told you about."

"I see; and was that young lady, who you also told me about, there?"

He blushed slightly. "Yes."

"Did you learn her name?"

He smiled, remembering the lilt of her voice when she said it. "Keiko."

"A pretty name."

"I think so."

His uncle's expression grew troubled as he

stood and came over to Jesse's desk.

"Be careful, Nephew. There are those who won't agree with your interest in a Japanese girl."

Though aware of the prejudice, he'd never experienced it himself. Jesse bore no resentment to the Japanese community, both because of his mother's insistence on equality, and the number of contracts *Sommers Management* had with Asian business owners. They rented many of the properties managed by the company, and he got along fine with them.

"I know, Uncle. There's nothing to be worried about right now, I'm not sure she even knows who I am, although she did remember my name."

"Did she now? Well, tread lightly; her family is likely to be wary of any outside influence on their daughter."

"I will, Uncle."

AUGUST, 1941

Jesse parked the sedan along the north side of Laguna and climbed out. August in San Francisco was usually breezy, but the temperatures hovered in the upper seventies or lower eighties. This day was no exception.

In short sleeves, he walked to the corner of Sutter, crossed the road, and into *Takeshi's.* It was just past lunchtime and the restaurant was half empty, many of the tables still covered with glasses, napkins, and plates of diners who had already left. He stood by the door, looking for Keiko, and waiting to be seated.

Just when he thought she might not be working, Jesse spotted her coming through the kitchen door, moving quickly in his direction.

He smiled broadly. "I would like my table, please."

Her smile was guarded. A man in the back booth seemed to be watching them. Jesse suspected it might be her father.

She picked up a menu. "This way."

He sat down in *his* booth, and refused the menu.

"The usual please."

Her smile remained subdued. "Very

good."

She left, and when she returned, it wasn't to his table. Instead, Keiko went to her station and kept her back turned toward him. Jesse wondered if he'd done something wrong.

A few minutes later, his soup arrived, set in front of him by a young girl who could've been Keiko's twin. He smiled at her. "Thank you."

"You're welcome." She quickly returned to the kitchen without speaking to Keiko.

Jesse ate his soup in silence, and Keiko never turned around to speak to him. She eventually returned to the kitchen. For whatever reason, she wasn't interested in talking to him, and he felt a little foolish staring after her.

He stood and went to the podium to pay his check. Keiko appeared suddenly in front of him. "Was everything okay, sir?"

His heart sank. *Sir?*

"Yes, everything was fine."

Jesse paid his check and she gave him his change without a smile.

As he went out onto the sidewalk, he found the day that only forty-five minutes ago was sunny, now seemed gray and depressing. He put his head down and headed for the car.

"Sir! Sir!"

He turned to see Keiko trotting after him.

"Sir, I shorted you some change."

When she got to him, Keiko put a quarter

in his hand. "Jesse?"

"Yes?"

She was staring directly into his eyes. "I hope you'll come back again—perhaps after two o'clock tomorrow?"

He met her gaze, and saw the pleading in her eyes. "After two?"

She nodded, smiled, and ran back to the restaurant.

Jesse watched after her until she disappeared, and then headed for the car.

The afternoon was suddenly pleasant again.

****

The next day, Keiko was especially hyper. She had all her paperwork done, all the tables cleared, and was standing by the podium when her father left.

"See you at five, Daughter."

"Yes, Father. Enjoy your nap."

When he was gone, Hotaru came up behind her. "What's up with you?"

"What do you mean?"

Her sister cocked her head sideways, letting her long hair fall to one side, and smirked.

"Father and Mother may not notice, but I can tell when you're nervous, and you are nervous!"

Keiko laughed. "Okay, maybe a little."

"I knew it. Why?"

Keiko looked around as if there might be a spy in the room. "You remember I told you Jesse came in yesterday."

"Sure."

"Well, Father was watching me very closely."

"Because he'd warned you about him."

"Exactly, so I had to act like I didn't care Jesse was there."

"Did Jesse know you were acting?"

Keiko's voice dropped as she fought the urge to burst into tears. "I don't think so, Roo."

"So you're afraid you'll never see him again?"

Keiko nodded. "I pretended he forgot his change and ran after him. I asked him to come by today after two."

"When Father goes to the house?"

"Yes."

They turned in unison to look at the clock on the wall. It read 2:10.

Rotating to look out the window, they stood quietly together, both hoping to see the young man with blue eyes.

"Girls, can you come into the kitchen?"

Keiko sighed. "Coming!"

After helping her mother get the dishes done, Keiko returned to the dining room. A glance at the clock told her it was now 2:45. She was trying to quell the panic rising inside when she noticed someone had seated themselves.

Keiko's face broke into a big smile as relief washed over her.

"Hello, Jesse."

"Hi, Keiko. I think I'll try some of those noodles you've been telling me about."

His smile sparked a surge in her pulse. "I think that's a very good idea. I'll put in your order and be right back."

"Swear?"

"Swear."

****

"You were right again, the noodles are magnificent."

Keiko stood at her station, facing Jesse. "My mother is a wonderful cook."

"What is your mother's name?"

"Azumi."

"That's pretty. What's your father's name?"

"Takeshi."

"Where is he now?"

"He's at home taking an afternoon nap."

"I see, and does he do this every day?"

"Yes."

"Does your mother rest also?"

Unable to control herself, she let annoyance spread across her face. "No. I tell her she needs to, but she won't."

Jesse stood to go. "Too bad. Please give her my compliments on the food."

"I will."

He paid and waited for his change. When she reached out, their hands touched. Keiko let hers rest there for a brief second and their eyes met.

Jesse grinned at her. "I believe I will begin taking my lunch a little later from now on, say after two o'clock."

She gave him a mischievous grin. "The service is much better at that time of the day."

"That settles it then. I'll see you later, Keiko."

"Swear?"

"Swear."

****

Hotaru nudged her sister. "He's here."

Keiko smiled. "I know."

"He's been here nearly every day for the last three weeks. Has he asked you out yet?"

"No."

"Why not?"

"Roo! That's none of your business."

Hotaru pouted. "I just want to know

what's going on. I don't have any excitement in my own life."

Keiko laughed. "Sorry, Roo, but you'll have to make your own magic."

"Magic? Is that what you call your feelings for Jesse?"

Keiko thought about it for a minute. "Yeah, I guess. Magic, fate, karma."

"Love?"

"It's too soon to call it love, Roo."

"Maybe so, but it sure looks like it from where I stand."

Keiko crossed the dining room toward her visitor, but before she reached Jesse's table, a boy stopped her. "Can I get some more to drink?"

"Of course." She went back to where Hotaru stood. "Can you give him a refill?"

"Sure."

Keiko finished her trip over to Jesse's table, smiling broadly. "The usual?"

"No thanks, I'm not hungry. I brought you a gift."

"Oh? What is it?"

"Close your eyes and open your hand."

Keiko did as instructed; something landed in her palm. When she opened her eyes, she was looking at a sand dollar seashell. "It's pretty."

"I found it out at China Beach."

She turned it over in her hand. She'd seen them before, but this one was a gift from Jesse.

"Where's China Beach?"

"Up near Seacliff. Do you know the area?"

"I think so."

He was watching her. "I like to go there to think. I find it peaceful."

"It sounds nice."

"Would you like to go with me sometime?"

Keiko looked into those blue eyes and weighed her response.

She very much wanted to say yes, but it meant crossing an invisible line drawn by her father. Still, her heart wouldn't let her head get in the way. "I think I'd like that."

"Great. What if we go while your father's resting tomorrow?"

"Okay, but we need to meet somewhere besides here."

Jesse nodded. "That's fine. Where?"

"I'll walk down Post Street and over to Octavia. Pick me up there at two-fifteen?"

"Perfect."

A commotion interrupted their conversation.

"Hey, leave me alone!"

Keiko turned to see her sister brush a boy's hand away from her leg. She went to her sister and pulled her aside. "What's the problem, Roo?"

"Mark insists on putting his hands where he shouldn't."

"You know him?"

"Yes, he goes to my school. His name is Mark Bowers."

Mark reached for Keiko. "What have we here? Are you the big sis?"

Keiko sidestepped his grasp and turned an icy stare on the boy.

"I think you should leave."

"Oh, come now, I haven't finished eating. What's your name?"

Keiko didn't know Jesse was beside her until he spoke.

"You heard the lady—it's time to leave."

Jesse stood over the boy, his muscles taut.

Mark appeared unfazed.

"This ain't no business of yours, Mister."

"That's where you're wrong. I just made it my business and I think you need to learn some manners. Now, are you leaving on your own, or am I helping you out the door?"

Mark hesitated, laughed nervously, then got up.

He was gone in less than five minutes.

Keiko sat at the booth with Jesse and thanked him twice. Hotaru came over as well.

"I'm Hotaru, Keiko calls me Roo."

Jesse smiled up at her from his seat. "Nice to meet you, Roo."

"Thanks for getting rid of Mark."

"It was nothing."

"Those boys only act like that to the

Japanese girls. They would never do that to the white cheerleader types."

Keiko turned on her sister. "Hotaru, don't be so crude."

Jesse held up his hand. "It's fine. Hotaru, don't ever let someone disrespect you. I don't care who they are." He stood. "I need to be going. See you tomorrow, Keiko?"

She blushed slightly and nodded. When he was gone, Roo ambushed her.

"Why did he ask if he would see you tomorrow?"

Keiko looked around to make sure no one was listening.

"We have a meeting set for tomorrow."

Roo squealed. "A date!"

Keiko put her hand over her sister's mouth. "Shush, Roo."

Roo mumbled from behind her sister's palm. "Oh…sorry. Mmmm…You have a date?"

"Not really. He's taking me for a walk on China Beach."

"Sounds like a date to me."

Keiko removed her hand and laughed.

"Yeah, I guess it sounds like a date to me, too."

****

The next afternoon, Keiko had all her

work done, and was out the door just past two. Roo was going to cover for her if their mother asked any questions. It wasn't uncommon for Keiko to take a walk during the lull in afternoon business, but she was rarely gone more than forty-five minutes to an hour.

The sun was bright and the breeze warm as she hurried along Post Street until she came to the corner of Octavia. Looking up and down the block, she hoped to see Jesse walking toward her, but she was one of only a few people there.

Her white sleeveless top ruffled in the breeze and some of her hair, which she had let out of its customary bun, caught in her mouth. As she pulled it loose from her teeth, a car horn startled her. Less than a half block down Octavia Street, a car door opened, and Jesse stepped out. He waved, beckoning her to meet him.

It was impossible for Keiko to miss the wide smile waiting for her as she approached. Jesse ran around to the passenger side and opened the door. She slid into the sedan, trying to calm the shaking of her hands and pounding of her heart. "Thank you."

"You're welcome."

He closed her door and flew around to his side, climbing in. "I'm glad you came."

She smiled but didn't look at him. "Me, too."

They drove in silence, and soon he pointed out the window. "There it is."

Keiko had never noticed the tiny strip of sand. It was a small cove, maybe two hundred yards long, and very private. They were the only ones there.

Jesse parked and opened her door. When he offered his hand, she accepted, letting him keep hold of her as he closed the door. He guided her down the set of steps that led to the small beach. Gulls flew away at their intrusion, but quickly returned to seek handouts from the new visitors.

Keiko laughed, then covered her mouth in embarrassment.

Jesse studied her. "What's funny?"

"The gulls. I think their walk is comical."

Jesse nodded. "Isn't it amazing how they can be so graceful in the air and so clumsy on the ground?"

She smiled softly. "I'm envious of creatures that fly. Birds, butterflies, even bees; they all seem so free when they soar."

"I feel the same away about sea creatures like the dolphin or whale. They make diving to incredible depths and leaping from the water look so easy."

Keiko bent down and picked up a sand dollar, brushing at it with her fingers. "I'll put this with the other one on my nightstand."

"Would you like to sit for a while?"

"That would be nice."

They used the bottom step as their bench. Staring out at the waves, they watched them lap at the shore. A never-ending parade of breaking ridges who found themselves pushed onto the shore, and then out of the way by the marchers coming in behind them. Keiko didn't remember ever feeling so peaceful.

Jesse broke the silence. "Did your father see you leave?"

"No, he had already gone."

"He would not approve?"

"Father does not approve of any boy showing an interest."

"Especially one who is not Japanese."

Though surprised by his candor, she refused to diminish the truth.

"Yes. Father is very traditional."

"What about your mother?"

Keiko realized she hadn't ever discussed boys with her mother, at least not pertaining to race, and she had to admit she wasn't sure.

"I don't know. If it came right down to it, I'm sure she would support Father, but I've never asked her."

Keiko turned toward Jesse. "What about you and your family?"

He hesitated before answering. "My dad died…"

"Oh, I'm sorry."

"It's okay. It was a few years ago. As for

my mother, I'm sure the only thing important to her is whether or not I'm happy."

They sat quietly for a long while, though to Keiko it seemed like just minutes. Eventually, Jesse stood and offered her his hand again.

"Come on. We need to get you back before your father returns."

Right now, Keiko didn't care what her father thought, but Jesse was only looking out for her. They walked to the car, close together but not quite touching. She relished his nearness, his smell, his quiet spirit, and his strength.

She wanted to stay longer, forever, but that wasn't realistic. She would have to wait for the next time they could be together and hope it would be soon.

When he dropped her off, he opened her door, then cleared his throat. "Uh, I had a nice time."

She looked straight into his eyes, not wanting her message to be missed. "I had a very nice time."

"Would you like to go again?"

"Very much."

His smile beamed down at her. "Great. When?"

"Tomorrow?"

"Same time?"

"Yes."

****

Jesse watched Keiko walk down Post Street until she disappeared around the corner. He didn't know how this would all turn out, but he couldn't imagine not seeing her again. His world was brighter when he was with her.

He turned to get back in the car when someone pushed him from behind. He landed on his knees, and when he looked up, four boys were standing around him. He recognized one of them immediately: Mark Bowers.

The other three boys were all bigger than Jesse, and they pushed in around him to make escape impossible.

Jesse tried to stay calm. "What's this about?"

Mark sneered at him. "Not so tough now, huh? I heard you makin' a date with that Jap girl yesterday. You're a Jap lover, aren't ya?"

"You don't want to do this, Mark."

Bowers grinned at his friends. "What do ya think? Is this what I want to do to a Jap lover?"

The three players laughed. "Yeah, you want to do it."

Mark looked down at Jesse, who hadn't tried to get up.

"Yes, Jap lover, I want to do this!"

They attacked all at once and Jesse could

only tuck himself into a fetal position, and hope it would be over quickly.

****

At just past two the next afternoon, Keiko arrived on the corner of Octavia and Post. Her hair was tied in a long braid, reaching almost to her waist, and she wore a light gray jacket that matched her pants. The breeze was cooler than the day before, but she barely noticed as she scanned the street for Jesse's car.

It wasn't where he'd parked the day before, and in fact, there were only four cars in the area. She checked the time. 2:10.

He must be running behind.

She stepped next to the building, finding a spot in the sun where she was protected from the wind. Watching each vehicle as it moved through the intersection, they all looked similar to his, but none was driven by Jesse. She looked down at her watch again. 2:20.

A horn blew and Keiko swirled in its direction, a smile bursting upon her face.

"Hey, beautiful! You want to take a ride with me?"

Keiko's smile vanished as she realized the car wasn't Jesse's. She turned away, not bothering to answer, and the car drove off.

Anxiety began to creep in on her, the

excitement of seeing Jesse replaced by a fear he wasn't coming. She checked the time again.

2:35!

The intersection had grown quiet. Keiko took one last glance along the street, then walked back to the restaurant. When she came through the door, Roo was immediately at her side.

"Why are you back so soon?"

"He didn't show up."

"What? Are you sure?"

She scowled at her sister. "Really? Of course, I'm sure."

"I don't understand. I thought you had a great time yesterday."

"I don't understand either, Roo."

Tears welled up in Keiko's eyes, and not wanting to cry in front of her sister, she excused herself. "I'm going home for a while."

"Are you okay?"

Keiko touched her sister's cheek. "I will be. Thanks."

FALL, 1941

The first several days after Jesse's no-show, Keiko watched the door from two until five each afternoon, but eventually she'd resigned herself to the reality of the situation. Something or someone had changed Jesse's mind about seeing her.

Lately, she'd hang around until about two-thirty, then take a walk. Usually, her walks were spent fighting back tears, and sometimes she even succeeded. Many of her walks were spent trying to find someone to blame.

Could Father be responsible? Did he discover the trip to China Beach?

While she didn't put it past her father to interfere, it seemed likely he would have confronted her.

And what about Mother? How did she feel about a non-Japanese suitor? Had she told Father about Jesse? Did she side with Father when he said he was going to put a stop to the relationship?

Deciding it was time to find out, she checked her watch; 3:05. There was still time to talk to her mother before either Roo or her father showed up. She pulled her coat tight against the October wind, and hurried back to the restaurant.

When she came through the door, her mother was sitting at the booth normally occupied by Father. Keiko removed her coat and got some tea, before sitting down across from her.

"Short walk today, Keiko. Is the wind cold?"

"A little."

Mother sat back in the booth and studied her. "Something troubles you, Daughter?""

"May I ask you a question, Mother?"

"Of course."

Keiko, suddenly unsure, met her mother's gaze. Keiko had inherited the same dark eyes as her mother's, but Azumi's were tired, almost faded. Keiko blamed her father.

"How…what…"

A tiny smile played at the corners of Azumi's mouth. "It's okay, Daughter."

Keiko took a deep breath, then spilled the question in a rush of air.

"Would you be okay with me seeing a boy who wasn't Japanese?"

Azumi didn't answer immediately, but cocked her head to one side, studying her daughter.

"You don't have any idea how I feel?"

An answer that was a question. Keiko shrugged. "I had never really thought about it until…" She stopped herself.

Her mother's eyebrows rose slightly. "Until *he* came around?"

Keiko blushed. "You saw him."

"I did. Does that tell you how I feel?"

"I guess so. Did you tell Father?"

Her mother let a mischievous grin take over her face.

"Now why would I do that?"

Keiko stood and hugged her mother.

"Thank you, although I guess it doesn't matter anymore."

"Oh?"

"I haven't seen Jesse in a while; I guess he changed his mind."

Azumi looked her daughter in the eye.

"I don't know what happened to your Jesse, but I know when a boy is crazy about a girl, and he is crazy about you."

Keiko wiped at her eyes. "You think so?"

Azumi touched her check gently. "I *know* so."

****

The next day, Roo came running through the back door of the restaurant. "Keiko! Keiko!"

"Up front, Roo."

Hotaru rushed up to where Keiko stood. "You'll never guess what happened at school today."

"I imagine you're right. Why don't you tell me?"

Her sister was bent over, attempting to catch her breath. When she started the story, her voice dropped to a whisper. "At the start of football practice today, the police showed up and arrested four of the players."

"Really? You were right, I wouldn't have guessed."

"There's more. One of them was Mark Bowers!"

"The kid who was bothering you a few weeks back?"

"Yes—the one Jesse kicked out of the restaurant."

"Why were they arrested?"

Roo fixed her sister with a chilling stare. "Assault and battery."

Keiko still wasn't sure why this was supposed to be such big news to her. "That's serious."

"Keiko, aren't you going to ask who they beat up?"

"Okay, who…" It struck her like a sledgehammer. "Jesse?"

"That's was my first thought."

"But you don't know for sure."

"No, but it happened a few weeks ago, and the victim was someone who didn't go to the school."

Keiko tried to imagine what kind of beating would cause Jesse to be gone so long. Thinking of him in pain, especially if it was because he helped Roo, brought on a wave of nausea. She sat down in Jesse's booth.

"How can we find out if it was him?"

"A reporter from the Chronicle was there; maybe we can find it in tomorrow's paper."

"That's a great idea, Roo."

Azumi came over to the table. "What's all the excitement about?"

Keiko looked up at her mother with wide eyes. "It turns out you may have been right about Jesse."

Azumi winked at her daughter. "I know it when I see it."

****

The next morning, Keiko was up early and headed to the corner store. She bought the morning's issue of the San Francisco Chronicle and returned home, locking herself in her bedroom. Spreading the paper out on her bed, she began to search.

The front page was filled with the usual stories about the war in Europe, as well as reports from Washington. Keiko rapidly flipped pages until she found the City section. At first, she didn't see it, but down in the bottom right corner was a small story.

FOUR FOOTBALL PLAYERS
ARRESTED AT LOCAL HIGH SCHOOL
All Four charged with Assault and Battery

Police arrested four young men at Abraham Lincoln High School yesterday afternoon. The juveniles, whose names are not being released, were charged in the beating of twenty-five-year-old Jesse Sommers.

Mr. Sommers had been in a coma at Saint Francis Memorial Hospital until coming out of it just three days ago. He was listed in stable condition and was able to tell police who had attacked him.

The four boys were arraigned before Judge Walter Curran, and then released to their parents. A trial date has not been set.

Keiko didn't know whether to cry for Jesse's pain or laugh with relief he hadn't stood her up. Saint Francis Memorial wasn't far from the restaurant. She would go there today.

****

Keiko was out the door by two-fifteen, and covered the eight blocks to the hospital in just a few minutes. The wind had let up, so she didn't need her coat, but the day was overcast. Saint Francis Hospital towered over her, pressing down from the sky, and tension engulfed her.

She entered the lobby from Hyde Street and went to the information desk. A pleasant lady in a blue hospital dress smiled as Keiko approached. "Can I help you?"

"Could you tell me what room Jesse Sommers is in?"

"Is that spelled with a U or an O?"

Keiko didn't know. "I'm not sure."

The lady laughed. "Well, it looks like it's an O. That's the only Sommers I've got. Room 211."

"Thank you."

Keiko, still in her work clothes and her hair in a bun, found her way up the stairs to the second floor. Following the room numbers until she got to 211, she stopped by the door. The room was actually a ward. Peering inside, she was distressed to see six beds, all of them occupied.

She let her gaze travel around the room, searching for Jesse, but most of the beds had curtains drawn around them. She froze, not sure what to do.

She couldn't go peeking around each curtain!

Then something she hadn't considered before crept into her consciousness.

What if he blames her? What if he doesn't want to see her?

Her feet seemed glued to the floor, but inside, she wanted to flee.

"Do you need help, Miss?"

Startled, Keiko spun to find a lady watching her from the nurse's station. Keiko crossed over to where the nurse sat. "I wanted to see Jesse Sommers."

"Oh, well, you have the right room."

"Which…which bed is his?"

"He's on the back right. Are you a friend of his?"

"Yes…well, actually, I'm an acquaintance."

The nurse, Marlene according to her nametag, smiled and came around the desk. "He's been sleeping a lot; let me see if he's awake."

Keiko waited while Marlene went into the room, returning a minute later. "He's asleep. Can I give him a message?"

Keiko played with the item in her pocket, unsure what to do. Finally, she took it out and handed it to the nurse. "Will you give this to him when he wakes up?"

"Of course. Who should I say left it?"

"Keiko."

"Alright, Keiko. I'll tell him you were here and left this for him."

"Thank you."

"You're welcome."

Keiko turned and hurried out of the hospital.

****

Jesse rolled over slowly. Unlike the first time he woke up, he recognized his surroundings, and remembered what happened. The pain had finally begun to subside, and other than the patch over his left eye, he looked pretty good for what he'd gone through.

"Hey, Sleepy."

Sitting in her usual spot, a chair at the bottom of his bed, his mother smiled at him. Her blonde hair was tied up in a ponytail, and she'd clearly not slept much. Her narrow face was even thinner now, and Jesse worried his mother hadn't been eating properly, either.

"Hi, Mom."

"How are you feeling?"

"Okay, I guess. My ribs have stopped throbbing—they were the worst."

"I imagine. Four of them were cracked by those animals."

Jesse studied his mother through his one good eye. "Are you getting any sleep?"

"Oh, I grab a few hours now and again."

"I'm worried about you. What about food? Are you eating?"

"I'm not hungry much."

"That's it! When do I get out of here?"

"Tomorrow, I think."

"Good, then we'll go out for a big dinner to celebrate!"

She smiled broadly. "It's a date. That reminds me. A young lady left this for you."

His mother laid a sand dollar shell in his hand. Jesse turned it over, his heart in his throat.

"When?"

"Earlier today. Apparently, you were asleep when she came by, so she left it with a nurse."

A smile played across his face as he examined the shell.

His mother studied him. "Who's Keiko?"

Jesse's smile widened considerably. "Someone special."

"I don't remember you mentioning her before. Isn't Keiko a Japanese name?"

Jesse's smile disappeared and he met his mother's gaze. "Is that okay?"

"Does she make you happy?"

"Yes, very much."

"Then I don't care if she's a penguin. If she makes you happy, I'm happy."

He laughed, and even though he was certain that would be her reaction, it was still a relief to hear it. "Thank you, Mother."

"How did you meet her?"

He laid the shell on his side table. "I

stopped to have lunch at a small restaurant that belongs to her family. She was the hostess."

"How long ago?"

"I'm not sure; six or eight weeks ago. I'm still a little foggy about time."

His mother's look turned serious. "There are those who won't like your interest in a Japanese girl."

"I know. In fact, I think that's why I was attacked."

"Jesse, you told me it was an attempted robbery."

"I know, and I'm sorry. You were already worried and I didn't want you thinking someone was after me."

"What about the police? Did you tell them the truth?"

"Yes. I had to."

His mother was quiet for a long time, and he could tell she was putting things together.

"Why did it happen?"

Jesse told her the whole story, and when he was done, he waited. After several minutes, his mother stood. "I need some air."

"Mom, please don't be angry."

"I'm not angry, I'm worried."

"There's nothing to be worried about."

"If you continue this relationship with Keiko, this may not be the last beating you get."

Jesse didn't know what to say. She was probably right, but it didn't matter, he missed

Keiko terribly. He watched his mother leave before he picked up the sand dollar and pressed it to his chest.

****

Keiko pulled on a light jacket and headed out for her afternoon walk. The day was sunny and cool as the calendar moved into late October, but she found the crisp air refreshing. When she reached the hospital, she went directly to the second floor, stopping in front of the big window at room 211.

Her heart sunk. The bed, where Jesse had been the day before, was now neatly made and empty. She turned to the nurse's station and spotted Marlene.

"Excuse me."

The nurse looked up and smiled. "Hi. Keiko, right?"

"Yes. Hello again."

"I gather you're looking for Mr. Sommers."

"Yes. Is he in a different room?"

"Mr. Sommers went home this morning."

"Oh…I see. Do you know if he got the shell?"

"He was carrying it with him when I wheeled him out."

Keiko couldn't conceal her joy, and her

face brightened instantly.

Marlene noticed. "He's a handsome young man."

Keiko blushed, not quite sure what to say. The nurse gave Keiko a knowing smile and a small wave. "Bye, Keiko. Good luck."

"Bye, and thank you."

Keiko made her way out of the hospital and took her time getting back to the restaurant. She didn't have any way to get hold of Jesse, and didn't know how soon he would be able to come by the restaurant.

One of her mother's favorite Japanese proverbs came to mind: *If you wait, it will come...just like fair weather.*

****

Three days later, the *fair weather* Keiko had been hoping for came through the restaurant door. Still wearing a patch over his left eye and limping slightly, Jesse gingerly slipped into his favorite seat.

Keiko was standing there before he settled in. "How are you?"

He looked up and smiled. "Better now that you're here."

She sat down opposite him, resisted the urge to take his hand, and scanned his face. "I am too."

"What?"

"Better now that you're here."

"Oh. I guess you're not mad at me for standing you up?"

Keiko tried to force an angry face over her smile. "Well, I'll tell you this much, it better not happen again!"

He laughed, then winced slightly.

Keiko winced with him. "I'm sorry, I didn't mean to make you hurt."

He waved his hand. "It's fine. It feels good to laugh again, despite the sore ribs."

"What about your eye? Will it be okay?"

Jesse shook his head. "Not really. I'll regain some sight in it, at least that's what the doctor thinks, but probably not more than fifty percent."

This time, Keiko did reach out for his hand, and he responded by clutching her fingers tightly.

A shadow suddenly loomed over the table. "Who is this, Keiko?"

Her mother stood next to them.

Keiko withdrew her hand. "This is Jesse Sommers. Jesse, this is my mother, Azumi."

"Nice to meet you, ma'am."

Azumi nodded at the young man, and then set a bowl of miso in front of him. "This one is on the house. I heard what you did for my daughter, and I am grateful to you."

Jesse seemed embarrassed, but pulled the

soup closer to him. "It was nothing."

Azumi gestured toward the eye patch. "It does not appear to have been *nothing*."

Jesse started eating the soup, and Azumi left them alone. When Jesse was done, he pushed the bowl away and nodded toward the kitchen.

"Your mother doesn't appear to mind you talking to me."

Keiko looked toward the kitchen, then back at Jesse. "No. I think she wants me happy, just like your mother does you."

Jesse reached into his pocket and produced the sand dollar. "It was wonderful to get this. It meant a lot to know you had come to the hospital."

"I'm glad, but it would have been nice of you to be awake!"

He laughed again, this time without the wincing. "Hey, it wasn't my fault. They were keeping me pretty drowsy."

Keiko's voice lowered as she remembered the weeks of wondering what happened to Jesse.

"I would have come sooner if I'd known about…"

"I know. Don't worry about it. How did you find out, anyway?"

"Roo came from school saying they arrested the boys. I kinda put two and two together, looked for the story in the paper, and found out where you were."

"Aren't you a smart one?"

She blushed. "I needed to know."

"Well, what about that date I owe you. Is it still something we can do?"

"Of course, if you're up to it."

"I am. Tomorrow?"

"Sure, but won't it be cold at the beach?"

"Probably, but we can still watch the waves from the car."

"That sounds perfect."

Her mother's voice came from the kitchen. "Keiko!"

She looked up, and Azumi nodded toward the door. Keiko sprung to her feet. "See you tomorrow."

"Okay."

Takeshi Yoshida came in, back from his rest early, and eyed Jesse as he passed by. Keiko pretended not to notice, and disappeared into the kitchen. When she came back out, Jesse was gone. She brought her father his Saki, and to her relief, he didn't ask any questions.

****

The next couple weeks fell into a regular pattern for Keiko. Each afternoon, after her father left, she would walk to where Jesse picked her up. Together, they'd drive to China Beach or some other private location.

Sometimes, if the sun was warm, they would walk while holding hands.

They had learned that certain spots were either not crowded, or people paid no attention to them. Marina Park, Hunter's Point, and Alta Plaza all served as safe places away from the prying eyes of both her father and people who might object.

When they wanted to have a meal, they would go to Fisherman's Wharf and mingle with the crowds, or sit at a wharf-side table. Sometimes, they would talk about the future, but mostly they just enjoyed each other's company.

The war in Europe was ever present in the news, and they discussed whether America would be drawn into the fight.

Jesse had indicated more than once that he would enlist. Keiko couldn't imagine him so far away for so long, but Jesse had reasoned that if he didn't enlist, he would be drafted anyway. Eventually, she would change the subject, secretly hoping it never happened.

As the first week of December drew to a close, Jesse picked her up, and drove to China Beach. The sun was out but the temperature was only in the fifties, so they remained in the car and watched the whitecaps on the bay. As he had several times before, Jesse put his arm around Keiko and drew her close.

He was quiet for a long time, and then

without warning, let his feelings tumble out too quickly. "If I have to go away to war, will you wait for me?"

Keiko was stunned, and tears welled up in her eyes.

She'd asked herself the same question many times. They'd been seeing each other for nearly six months now, and Keiko had let herself begin to imagine a future with Jesse. She would face her father down when the time came, confident in her mother's support, and sure of her own feelings.

Still, in all her dreaming, it was always in the future when the decision had to be made. Now she wondered if Jesse was trying to tell her something.

Had he enlisted already? Would he be gone soon?

Her heart pounded as she looked up at him, his eyes gazing down at her expectantly. There was only one answer. "Yes."

Tears appeared on his cheeks. "Are you sure?"

She nodded, and his relief was obvious. He leaned over and pressed his lips to hers.

His kiss was firm but not hard, and she let her arms reach around his neck, pulling her body closer to him. The kiss lasted for both an eternity and a split second, and when he pulled back, she buried her face in his neck.

They stayed like that until he looked at his

watch. “We need to get you back.”

She forced herself over to her side of the car, wiping at her face, and trying to quiet her pulse. She’d had the occasional kiss in her high school years, but nothing like the thrill and emotion of a kiss shared with Jesse. The conviction of her answer was unwavering; she would wait if she had to, for as long as she had to.

DECEMBER 7, 1941

Sunday was the only day of the week when Keiko could sleep in. She crawled out of bed this day at 10:30 and made her way into the kitchen.

Hotaru was already at the table eating. "Good morning. How was your date with Jesse yesterday?"

Keiko looked quickly around for her father. Roo pointed over her shoulder. Her mother and father were sitting at a small table in the back yard. She relaxed and smiled.

"It was wonderful. He asked me if I would wait."

"Wait for what?"

"For him, if he had to go to war."

Roo took another bite. "Oh… Let's hope that isn't necessary."

"Believe me, I am."

"It sounds like you two are serious. Have you talked about marriage?"

Keiko rolled her eyes. "You mean have we talked about how to get married without father killing Jesse?"

Roo laughed. "Yeah, that."

"Not really. It's been there under the surface, but nothing has been said. I think his question last night was a prelude to discussing it."

"I think it would be awesome."

Keiko stood up to get dressed. "Me, too."

In her room, she tidied up some, then put on slacks and a white, button-down shirt. She was just about to brush her teeth when a commotion outside the bathroom window caught her attention.

A few seconds later, her father's voice boomed through the house. "Keiko! Hotaru!"

When she came out of the bathroom, her father and mother were rushing in through the back door. Roo was frozen in place, a bite of food half way to her mouth.

The fear on her mother's face was unmistakable. Takeshi brushed past both his daughters.

"Follow me!"

The three women trailed him into the living room, where they found him playing with the radio. As he got it tuned, the news blared across the house.

"We have witnessed this morning an attack on Hawaii, and a furious bombing of the Pearl Harbor Naval Station by fighter planes, undoubtedly Japanese. The city of Honolulu has also been attacked and considerable damage done. The main targets in this action by the Japanese appear to be Hickman Field and the great naval base at Pearl Harbor."

"Firemen and policemen have been called up to be stationed in certain locations on the islands to make sure there is no revolutionary activity by Japanese residents who may be rendering assistance to the attacking force. Fifty to one-hundred planes, bearing the Rising Sun emblem on their wings, were said to have carried out this attack."

The news reports continued almost non-stop but Keiko had already tuned out, instead focusing on her mother. Where her father was animated, wiping his brow, smacking his knee, and occasionally uttering a cuss word or two, Azumi was motionless. Her expression blank, her eyes unmoving, to the point Keiko wasn't sure if her mother was still breathing.

"Mother?"

No response. Keiko touched her shoulder. "Mother, are you okay?"

Azumi still didn't move, but when she spoke, her words frightened Keiko.

"Things will never be the same."

"What do you mean?"

Her mother's words were barely above a whisper. "Why would Japan do such a thing? A sneak attack is dishonorable."

Keiko was trying to catch up. "How will things change?"

Azumi didn't seem to hear her, and Keiko was distracted by a noise outside. "Takeshi!"

Her father went to the front door, opening it just a crack. "Yes?"

"You better get down to the restaurant."

"Why?"

Keiko recognized the voice of their neighbor, Mr. Ito. "The windows have been smashed in."

Takeshi turned to look at Azumi. "Don't…open…this…door…until…I…return."

His wife nodded without looking at him.

Keiko stood. "Father, do you wish me to go with you?"

"No. Stay with your mother, lock the door behind me, and remain inside."

He left, slamming the door behind him.

Keiko crossed the room and snapped the lock shut.

****

After Jesse and his mother got back to their house, they listened to the initial reports coming from Hawaii until his uncle called to check on them, and suggested they come over for dinner.

"Do you want to go, Mom?"

Estelle Sommers had been quiet since hearing the news in church, and despite several attempts, Jesse had not been able to draw her into a conversation. She would look at him and smile weakly, then go back to her daydreaming. She did the same now.

"Thanks Uncle Jerry, but I don't think Mom feels like going anywhere."

"Okay, but if you change your mind, we've got lots of food."

"Will you be going to the office tomorrow?"

There was silence on the phone, followed by his uncle clearing his throat. "I…imagine so. Unless something else happens, I gather business will go on."

"I'll see you then."

"That's fine, but Jesse…"

"Yes?"

"Make sure your mother is okay before coming in."

"I will. Uncle Jerry, what do you think…"

"I don't know, Jesse. I doubt even the president knows what happens next."

Jesse set the phone down as his mother turned the radio up for the tenth time, as if changing the volume might change the story.

"A second attack has occurred on the naval and army bases at Manila in the Philippines. These attacks followed the bombing of Pearl Harbor. President Roosevelt has called his advisors to the White House and is still receiving updates."

He walked over and sat down next to her. "Are you okay, Mom?"

She laid her hand on his, smiled, and nodded. "I'm fine. I just want to continue praying for our boys."

"I know Aunt Martha will appreciate it."

"I'm not just praying for my nephews—all our boys need prayers today."

Jesse finally understood why she'd been so quiet. Her burden was for all the men under fire at this very moment. They all were her boys today.

His thoughts returned to Keiko.

What must she be feeling? What is her family thinking? They must be frightened and maybe even feel like enemies on foreign soil.

Jesse found it difficult to think of them as the enemy. Keiko, Roo, Azumi, and many of the other Japanese he interacted with on a daily basis, were some of the nicest people he'd ever met.

He wanted to find Keiko, check on her, tell her it was going to be all right, that *they* would be all right. But he didn't know that, did he. In fact, he had to admit he wasn't sure about anything now.

The world had just stopped spinning, and everyone's lives had be thrown into an abyss called the unknown, where most everything would be changed forever.

"Mother?"

She looked up at him, her eyes contradicting the smile she attempted, and seemed to sense what was on his heart. She patted his hand gently. "I'll be fine. You go check on your Keiko."

He hesitated. "Are you…"

She patted his hand again, this time a little firmer. "Go on! I'll be okay."

He stood, kissed the top of her head, and moved to the door.

"Thank you. I'll be back soon."

As he shut the door, her eyes closed again, and her lips restarted their silent movement.

****

Keiko and Roo had sat huddled together on the couch opposite their mother. Azumi was lost in her own thoughts, leaving the girls to spend the past couple hours alternating between listening for noise outside and news reports on the radio.

Keiko nudged her sister. "You hear anything?"

"No. It's so still out there, it's scary."

"I know."

Keiko moved to the window for the hundredth time, pulling the drape back slightly to search for her father. The streets were empty—everyone apparently hunkered down out of sight. She was on her way back to the couch when the doorknob rattled.

Both sisters stopped, their eyes transfixed on the front door. The knob moved again and the door burst open. Their father came in, shutting the door quickly behind him. Despite rarely showing affection to their father, they ran and hugged him, relieved he was back.

"It's okay, girls. How's your mother?"

He released his daughters and walked over to Azumi. Their father bent over, touched her shoulder, and said something into her ear. When he stood up again, she gave him a small smile.

Roo had returned to the couch. "What's going on out there, Father?"

Tension played across his face. "The streets are pretty quiet. Most people I talked to, Japanese and otherwise, seem to be in shock."

Keiko sat next to her mother. "How's the restaurant?"

"It's fine. Somebody tossed a rock through the front glass, but I boarded it up. Have you been listening to the radio?"

"Sometimes, but when it gets overwhelming, we shut it off."

"I'm going to turn it back on. Why don't you girls get some dinner started?"

Keiko and Roo got up, grateful for something to do, and left the room. News reports came on in the other room, but in the kitchen, they were muffled. That suited Keiko just fine.

****

There was very little traffic to slow Jesse down, and within a few minutes, he was parked in front of *Takeshi's*. A large board was nailed up over the front window, and the sidewalk in front was strewn with broken glass. Two other businesses on the block were boarded up in the same manner.

Jesse didn't know where Keiko lived, and he'd hoped she might be at the restaurant. He sat for a long time, not sure if he was waiting for Keiko to show up, or because this was as close to her as he could get at the moment. It was probably a combination of the two.

An idea came to him, so he started the car, and drove three blocks over. Stopping in the spot where he usually picked Keiko up each day, he searched for her tiny form in the growing shadows.

Slowly, the sun disappeared, and he became aware of the growing darkness. Worried about his mother, he started the car, reluctantly acknowledging Keiko wasn't going to show up. He pulled away from the curb and headed for home.

The streets appeared darker than normal. Were there fewer lights on, or was it a sense of foreboding that shrouded the city?

Eventually he realized most porches were dark, front window drapes were drawn tight, and only an occasional streetlight shined in the night.

Folks were scared. He could hardly blame them. He was scared, too.

****

That night, fear engulfed the Japanese community. The Yoshida's, like most Japanese residents of the west coast, stayed inside with the lights off. In the darkness of their home, Roo was afraid to go to school the next day, Keiko worried about the impact on her relationship with Jesse, and Azumi feared for her husband and the rest of the Japanese-American community.

Keiko didn't sense fear in her father, but something else.

His manic behavior of the afternoon had morphed into a reserved sadness. Throughout the day, he'd spoken on the phone in hushed tones. When he hung up, his head would slowly rotate back and forth, and he'd return to sit next to Mother.

Keiko had prodded him, wanting to understand.

"You seem sad, Father."

His eyes had met hers, then dropped away.

"It is grief you see, Daughter."

"Grief, Father?"

"Yes. I am grieving for our country, and the shame it has brought upon us and all Japanese people."

Keiko's brow furrowed. "Shame? I don't understand."

"It is said that an honorable samurai will never strike with his sword to an opponent's back."

"The surprise, Father?"

"Yes. I fear the sneak attack will bring consequences far graver than any declaration of war."

Keiko ached for her father, who seemed buried beneath a burden she could only partially understand. But for the first time, she realized her father had a softer side, and his love for both Azumi and his family, was powerful.

****

Jesse arrived home to find his mother on the phone. She smiled at him, but her conversation was hushed, and he couldn't make out who she was talking to. After going to the kitchen for a glass of water, he returned to find she'd hung up.

"Who was that?"

"Your Aunt Martha."

"Has she heard—"

Estelle shook her head. "Not yet, but her boys were both on the *Arizona*."

"I heard it was hit hard."

"She is hoping for the best."

"You turned the radio off; nothing new?"

"Not really. They keep saying the same things over and over."

He sat next to her on the couch. "I think we could all use some quiet."

"Did you find Keiko?"

When he shook his head, she laid her head against his shoulder. "I'm sure she's fine."

They were quiet for a while, then she looked up at him. "I'm afraid, Jesse."

Jesse put his arm around her. "Me, too. I think everyone is."

DECEMBER 8, 1941

When Jesse arrived at the office the next day, Janet wasn't there, and his uncle was on the phone. Jesse put his things on his desk and got a cup of coffee. Jerry was just hanging up when he returned. "That was Janet; she said she needed a couple days off."

Jesse sat at his desk and leaned back in his chair. "Is she okay?"

"She's not sick, if that's what you mean, but she has three brothers in the military. One was already in Manila and they haven't heard from him. The other two have been called up to immediate duty."

"Reports say all leave has been cancelled and men were to report to their units ASAP."

"Yeah, so her brothers are gone. She wants to be with her folks."

"Easy to understand. I imagine everyone is in shock this morning."

His uncle got up to refill his own coffee cup as the phone rang. Jesse reached for it.

"Sommers Management."

"Hi, Jesse. Is Jerry there?" It was his Aunt Carol.

"He's getting coffee. How are you holding

up?"

She started to answer but choked up.

When his uncle returned, Jesse held out the phone to him. "It's Carol."

"Hello?"

Jesse couldn't hear his aunt, but the impact of her words on his uncle was clear. "Are they sure?"

Jesse watched intently as his uncle squeezed his eyes closed. "Okay, I'll be home early."

He handed the phone back to Jesse. "Our neighbors, the Carters, got word this morning that their son died on the *Oklahoma.* He was twenty."

The office fell silent and each man retreated to his own thoughts. Finally, Jerry stood and went over to the radio. He hesitated, then reached for the knob. News reports filled the office.

"The country of Japan has declared war on the United States after the surprise attack on Pearl Harbor yesterday. Congress will convene today at noon eastern time, to hear from President Roosevelt, and to draft a formal answer to Japan."

Jesse stood, dumped his coffee, and headed for the door. "I won't be in the office for a while, Uncle."

"Where are you going?"
"I have something I need to do."

****

Keiko made sure Roo got off to school without any problem, then went to the restaurant. The board over the window was unsettling, but her father had painted the word *OPEN* across it.

The activity around the restaurant seemed like any other day, except no one was smiling. Even the sun seemed a little dimmer.

In the kitchen, her mother was busy preparing food, having regained some of her energy. Keiko was glad to have something other than news reports to focus on, and her mother seemed to feel the same way.

Father sat in his booth with some paperwork in front of him. Repeatedly, he would look up to scan the front sidewalk, then go back to his work. Finally, he gathered the paper and pushed it aside. "Unlock the door, Keiko."

"Yes, Father."

As she turned the lock, one of their regulars approached the door. Mr. Sanders, the owner of an insurance agency, was there for his usual early lunch. "Good morning, Keiko."

"Good morning, Mr. Sanders."

He went to his favorite table, and Keiko found herself relieved there wasn't animosity in his tone. The rest of the lunch rush went the same way. Both Japanese and non-Japanese customers came, many quieter than usual, speaking in hushed tones rather than the normal boisterous carrying on.

Keiko was grateful she didn't sense any tension in the regulars. She dared to hope they wouldn't be blamed for what Japan had done.

Her father had made a point to speak to every customer. Moving around the diner, pausing at each table, inquiring about family members, or saying thanks for coming in. When the lunch rush slowed and it came time for him to go home, he remained seated at the back booth.

It didn't matter; Keiko had to see if Jesse would be at their usual spot.

She waved at her mother before turning to her father. "I'm going for a walk."

"Keiko."

Her heart skipped a beat. "Yes?"

"Be careful, and don't be gone long."

"Yes, Father."

She allowed herself a sigh of relief as she went out the door.

Hurrying without running, she headed to their normal rendezvous. Her pulse surged when she spotted Jesse sitting in his car. Climbing in, she smiled, and kissed his cheek. His response was to start the car and drive.

Keiko sat quietly until she couldn't stand it anymore. "Are you angry with me?"

"No."

"Then why are you not speaking to me?"

He pulled the car into a small parking lot near Alta Plaza, a four-square block area overlooking Fort Mason, the Presidio, and Alcatraz. They sat in silence for several minutes, watching the waves on the bay, and the now frantic pace at Fort Mason. Men and equipment were moving in random directions at breakneck speed.

Finally, Jesse reached across and took her hand. His face softened, and when he spoke, his voice was low and husky.

"I'm sorry, Keiko. I'm not mad at you."

She stared into his eyes. "I was afraid you blamed me."

"For the attacks—of course not. It's something else."

She reached up, touching his cheek, and could almost feel pain radiating from him. "What is it? Is your family okay?"

"Yes. They're okay for now, but in shock like everyone else."

"I'm sure. What is it then?"

He turned away, dropping her hand, and stared out the driver's window. His words struck the glass and reflected back to her.

"I went to enlist in the Navy this

morning."

Keiko stopped breathing. "You're going away?"

He shook his head.

"What then?"

"I was rejected. They wouldn't take me."

She was stunned. To her this was wonderful news, and his sorrow was confusing.

"You're not going away?"

Jesse shook his head again, still not looking at her. "No."

"Why did they not accept you?"

"The damage to my eye—my vision was too compromised."

She leaned back in her seat, watching the birds land on the plaza, while trying to make sense of the contradiction between her feelings and Jesse's.

She was relieved, even thrilled, to find out he wouldn't be going away. But Jesse was clearly upset at not being able to enlist. Why would he *want* to go to war? Maybe his feelings for her had changed because of the attack.

Jesse turned to look at her, his voice rising. "Don't you understand?"

"No, I guess I don't. I'm relieved you're not going away to be killed."

"It's my duty, and my obligation, as an American to fight. It's an honor to serve my country, and that honor has been denied me because of my eye!"

His words rocked her.

His standing up for Roo had caused his injury. In a bizarre twist, she realized his protection of a Japanese-American girl meant he couldn't go fight the Japanese for America.

Her head spun and she thought she would vomit.

"I'm…sorry. I didn't realize."

"It's not your fault. I shouldn't have yelled at you."

She nodded and they sat quietly, until Keiko spoke.

"I need to get back. Father didn't leave the restaurant today."

Without speaking, Jesse started the car and returned to their drop-off spot. When she got out, she came around to his side of the car.

He opened the window. "Keiko?"

Her brown eyes looked into his. "Yes?"

"You said you'd wait for me."

She nodded.

"I am glad you won't have to suffer through that."

She kissed his cheek. "I am too."

****

Roo was sitting on a bench in front of the restaurant when Keiko got back. "Did you see him?"

"Yes."

"How did it go?"

"It was strange at first. Something was bothering him and he wouldn't tell me what it was."

Roo stared at her as if she were daft. "Our people just bombed his country. What's hard to understand?"

"It wasn't that."

"What then?"

"He tried to enlist and they wouldn't take him."

"Oh. Well, that's good, right?"

"I thought so, but not to Jesse. He wanted to serve his country."

"Wait, why wouldn't they take him?"

"When Mark Bowers and his buddies attacked him, the damage they did to his eye was too severe. Jesse was rejected."

Keiko could see recognition on her sister's face. Roo grasped the implications faster than she had. "Does he blame us?"

Keiko shook her head. "No. I imagine he blames Bowers."

"I feel bad for Jesse, but I am glad for you, Sister."

Keiko hugged her. "Thanks. What about you? How was school?"

"Okay, I guess. There wasn't anything said, no fights or anything like that, but most of the Japanese kids stayed together."

"I imagine it was frightening."

"A little, but the other kids didn't seem to blame us. At least, not yet."

****

Roo had gone to the house to do her schoolwork, and Keiko was cleaning tables after dinner, when the phone rang. She crossed to the desk and picked it up. "Takeshi's"

"Yes, is Takeshi there?"

"Hold, please."

She laid the phone down and called to the back booth. "For you, Father."

She returned to her work but could hear her father's side of the conversation. "When?"

A moment's silence, then: "Who was it?"

Keiko slowed her cleaning, listening intently.

"Thank you for calling me."

Her father hung up and went to the kitchen. When he came back out, he was wearing his coat, and left without a word. Her mother came out of the kitchen and went to where her father had been sitting. After gathering up his paperwork, she made her way toward the kitchen. She paused to look at Keiko. "Will you be done soon, Daughter?"

"Yes, Mother."

Ten minutes later, they locked up the

restaurant and left for home.

Keiko and her mother arrived to find Roo sitting in the living room, her eyes red from crying. Azumi looked down at her daughter. "Where's your father?"

"In the backyard."

Azumi went through the kitchen and out the back door. Keiko sat down next to her sister. "What's wrong, Roo?"

"He's burning everything!"

"Burning? What are you talking about?"

"He came through the door a little while ago and started rummaging through the house. He took anything written in Japanese and threw it in a pile out back."

"Why?"

"I don't know, but when I asked him, he said it was necessary. Then he set the pile on fire."

Keiko looked through the glass of the back door. A flickering orange glow illuminated the kitchen interior. She struggled to control the fear building inside her as she put her arm around Roo, and together they watched the flame through the glass grow, then subside.

Almost an hour later, their mother and father came back inside. The ash on her father's face was muddied by sweat, and her mother's eyes were puffy from crying. They came into the living room and sat across from their daughters.

Keiko went to the bathroom and brought her father a towel. He nodded his thanks, sighed, and tried to explain. His words came slowly, as if exhaustion would steal his voice if he spoke too quickly.

"I got a call at the restaurant tonight from Mr. Ito. He said the FBI had arrested three of our neighbors from the next block over. He warned me that people in the Japanese-American community are being advised to rid themselves of anything that would indicate support for our home country."

Keiko's brow furrowed. "Who is advising this?"

"Leaders in the Japanese-American Citizens League."

"The JACL? But, surely the FBI doesn't think somebody in San Francisco helped with an attack a thousand miles away?"

"I don't know. However, they could fear we may assist in an attack here."

Keiko was incredulous. "But we are Americans. Why would we help with the destruction of our homes?"

Her father nodded. "I understand, Daughter. Fear is a powerful thing, and people are afraid."

Keiko caught sight of gaps on the bookshelf. "Where's the family album?"

Her father seemed unable to answer, and her mother spoke so softly, Keiko missed her answer.

Roo had heard. "Burned it?"

Azumi nodded.

Keiko looked from Roo to her mother. "You burned our family album?"

"It had to be done."

"Why? Why did it have to be done?"

"Because of the war; which side we support must be clear. All books with Japanese writing had to be burned."

Keiko jumped up and ran to the backyard. The album's edge stuck out from beneath the ashes and she reached for it. Just the corner came away from the smoldering embers. The ornately drawn letter 'Y' stared back at her, but everything inside was gone.

She threw the piece back on the fire and collapsed to the ground, drawing her knees up under her chin. Her tears were reflected in the glowing embers.

****

That evening, Jesse came home to a dark house. Coming through the front door, he was met by the sound of the news report on the radio.

"A Times Washington correspondent has reported that the Government of the United

States expects Germany and Italy to declare war on the US within hours. This follows the announcement by Sir Winston Churchill that Britain has declared war on Japan."

He flipped the light on and found his mother sitting in the dark, her eyes red. "Mom, what is it?"

"I got a phone call from your Aunt Martha a little while ago."

He turned off the radio as a lump formed in his throat. "What did she say?"

"Both your cousins died in the attack."

Jesse dropped down on the couch next to his mother. "Oh, no. That's terrible. How is she holding up?"

"About how you'd expect."

Jesse put his arm around her, and they sat in the quiet for a long time. Eventually, she turned to him. "Did you hear the president's speech to Congress?"

"I did. War has finally come to our shores, I'm afraid."

She searched his eyes. "Will you have to go?"

"I wanted to."

"*Wanted* to?"

"Yes. I tried to enlist in the Navy today."

"What happened?"

"I was denied."

She touched the scar near his eye.

"Because of this?"

He nodded.

"I know you want to serve your country, but you're all I have left."

"Have you told Keiko?"

"Yes. She feels the same way as you."

"It's because we love you."

He gave her a weak smile, torn inside between his desire to fight, and the women in his life being glad he couldn't. "I know."

"How is she?"

He shrugged. "Worried, afraid, shaken."

"Japanese or not, that describes all of us."

He kissed her forehead and got up, turning the radio back on. "I'm going to bed. Don't stay up all night listening to the news."

"I won't. I love you, Son."

"I love you too, Mother."

CHRISTMAS, 1941

Christmas and New Year's came and went, barely acknowledged. America was getting ready for war, and it consumed most people's time, as well as their conversations. Keiko and Jesse were able to get away for part of Christmas Eve and exchange small gifts, but mostly they ignored the holidays.

Keiko found life most normal at the restaurant. People she'd known as regulars still came to eat her mother's cooking, but slowly the enlisting of young men into the military was aging the clientele. Most of the young men who still came in to eat were obviously handicapped in some way that prevented their enlistment.

A limp, a physical deformity, or some ailment that disqualified someone from service, meant these men were left behind. A stigma attached itself to them, regardless whether they *wanted* to go or not, somehow branding them as less than a man.

Keiko sensed it in Jesse, and tried to bring it up once when they were sitting at China Beach.

"Are you okay, Jesse?"

"Sure, why?"

"There was a young man in the restaurant today who was crying."

"Oh?"

"His girlfriend was telling him not to be ashamed at being listed as 4F."

Jesse looked away.

"I understand how he feels."

She reached for his hand. "It's not your fault, you know that."

"I know, but somehow it doesn't matter."

Other signs of war would occur, sometimes in unexpected ways. One day, Keiko's father came into the restaurant later than normal and went directly to Azumi. He whispered something to her, then left again, carrying a pair of binoculars that sat on a shelf in the kitchen. Two hours later he returned with a somber look on his face.

"What is it, Father?"

"I am sorry Keiko, but I had to turn your camera in to the Defense Command."

"My camera? Why?"

"By orders of the government. All cameras, binoculars, shortwave radios, and radio transmitters must be turned in. It was posted at the Japanese community center."

"But that is my property."

"I'm sorry, Daughter. They said you will get it back eventually."

Keiko was both angry and afraid. Angry for being singled out because she was Japanese, and afraid, for owning something considered a threat to America. Each new declaration seemed to reduce their sense of safety and belonging.

There was no point arguing with her father. He was only doing what he must to try and keep them safe. Most of the other leaders in the community had already been questioned, and some arrested. So far, Takeshi had avoided the same fate, maybe because so many Caucasians ate at the restaurant.

Either way, Keiko had already learned that the saying common to most Japanese these days was painfully true.

"Shikata ga nai" - It cannot be helped.

****

Early in the new year, Jesse arrived at the office one day to find a newspaper sitting on his desk. The headline screamed at him:

OUSTER OF WEST COAST JAPANESE

EXPECTED SOON

Jesse dropped into his chair and read the story beneath the headline.

The entire California, Washington and Oregon coastal region, as well as the southern sections of California and Arizona along the

Mexican border, today were designated Military Area No. 1 by Lieut. Gen. John L. DeWitt, commanding the Western Defense Command and Fourth Army.

While no immediate evacuation order was issued, General DeWitt suggested all Japanese—alien and American-born—might do well to get out of Military Area No. 1 as quickly as possible.

"Those Japanese and other aliens who move into the interior out of this area now will gain considerable advantage and in all probability will not again be disturbed," he said.

Creation of Military Area No. 1 eventually will clear all American-born and alien Japanese and hundreds of other enemy aliens from the coastal section of California in which are located the most important military and industrial establishments. San Francisco and the entire Bay Region as far as Vallejo and Tracy are within the prohibited zone.

The proclamation and the specific evacuation orders, which are to follow "shortly," are culmination of an alien control policy the government instituted immediately after the attack on Pearl Harbor.

Disgusted, Jesse threw the paper onto the desk. Thousands of Japanese and Japanese-Americans were being punished for the actions of a government that no longer represented them. And that included Keiko.

The front door opened and Uncle Jerry came storming in. He threw a folder on his desk and went to fill his coffee cup. When he returned, he paced the office while on a rant at no one in particular.

"Those idiots! Don't they know I can't just throw tenants out? They have a lease that gives them a legal right to be there!"

Jesse leaned back in his chair and regarded his uncle. It appeared everybody was losing their minds. "What is it, Uncle?"

Jerry turned and looked at him, apparently noticing for the first time that anyone was in the office. "Larry Nixon—you remember him?"

"Sure, we handle several of his properties."

"Well, not for long!"

"Why?"

Jerry reached onto his desk and grabbed the folder, tossing it to Jesse.

"Read for yourself."

Jesse opened the folder and scanned the top sheet.

Jerry Sommers
Sommers Property Management

Dear Jerry,

Please be informed that I wish to have all tenants of Japanese descent removed from my properties. Inform them that their lease has been revoked and they must vacate within five days.

Sincerely,
Larry Nixon

Jesse looked up at his uncle. "We can't do that."

His uncle resumed his pacing. "That's what I told him. They have the legal right to be there unless they break the terms of their lease. Do you know what he said?"

Jesse shook his head.

"He said he didn't care about the legalities of it, he didn't want to be seen as supporting the enemy!"

A chill ran down Jesse's spine. Paranoia was becoming rampant. "That's ridiculous."

Jerry dropped into his chair. "That's what I told him. He said he didn't care, and if I wouldn't do it, he would find another property management company who would."

"He can't do that either. He's under contract to us."

Jerry ran his hand through his hair and sighed. "That's exactly what I said."

"So, what happens now?"

"Well, I'm not throwing anyone out, and

we'll just have to hope he comes to his senses sooner rather than later."

Jesse got up to get his own cup of coffee. "Everyone is going a little nuts. There's a lot of fear in the air."

When Jesse returned with his coffee, Jerry looked up from reading the front-page article. "They're recommending the Japanese community get out while the getting's good."

"It looks that way. The problem for most is where to go."

Jerry dropped the paper on the desk. "What about Keiko's family? Are they going to leave voluntarily?"

"I don't know, Uncle. I don't know."

****

Keiko was late getting away that afternoon, but Jesse was waiting for her when she got to their corner. She climbed into the sedan and kissed his cheek as they pulled away. They made small talk and held hands as they drove to China Beach. The weather was still a little too cool to sit by the water, but Keiko was okay with moving over next to Jesse and laying her head on his shoulder.

Usually, she would listen to him breathe as they spent this time quietly, just glad to be together for a few hours. Today, Jesse leaned back and fixed her with a worried look. "Has your father decided what he's gonna do?"

"You mean about leaving?"

"Yeah."

She shook her head. "He won't go. Unless he's forced out, he'll stay with his restaurant."

"How about your mother?"

"She doesn't say much about leaving. In fact, she doesn't speak much at all lately. She just focuses on cooking the food and keeping the restaurant going."

Jesse was quiet for a long time. Finally, he reached up and brushed her cheek, pushing a stray hair from her face. "Will you go with them if they leave?"

"I imagine I'll have to."

"But you're Nisei; doesn't that matter?"

The question surprised her. She hadn't considered the idea, but something her father had said came back to her.

He had been arguing with some men from the JACL.

"But they're born here, why must they go?"

"The War Department isn't differentiating between Issei and Nisei. They say all are Japanese."

Her father slammed his fist on the table. "It's ridiculous! They were born in America! This is their home."

Her parents were Issei, Japanese for 'first

generation,' which described those who emigrated from Japan. Keiko and Roo were Nisei, or 'second generation,' and had been born in America. It didn't matter to some people.

"I'm sorry Jesse, but even if I *was* allowed to stay, I must go with my family."

He looked away.

Things had come full circle.

Jesse would not be going away, but she might. Where or for how long was impossible to know.

"Jesse?"

He remained turned away. "Yes."

"Will you wait for me?"

Keiko held her breath while the question hovered in the space between them. After a few seconds, he looked back, tears rolling down his cheeks.

"I love you, Keiko. I'll wait for you just as you would've waited for me."

****

February nineteenth was like any other morning since the war started until Jesse got to his desk. The newspaper was laid out, the headline blaring at him.

ENEMY ALIENS TO BE MOVED FROM COASTAL AREAS

He swung around to see both Janet and his uncle watching him.

"Does that mean what I think it does?"

Jerry stood, laid his hand on his nephew's shoulder.

"It happened last night. President Roosevelt signed an Executive Order calling for military exclusion zones, and the removal of certain people from those areas."

Jesse grabbed the paper and read the story. It said orders to evacuate will be coming soon, and those affected should take steps to be prepared.

Despair washed over him.

Keiko would be leaving. What would he do without her?

He threw the paper into the trashcan and left the office. When he got to *Takeshi's*, a small crowd had formed outside, and the newspaper was being passed around.

Jesse pushed past them and found Keiko sitting at his booth. "Are you okay?"

Her eyes were red. "They're going to force us out."

He sat down across from her, reaching for her hand, not caring if her father was around.

"When? Do you know?"

She shook her head.

"Do *you* have to go?"

"It doesn't say only Issei, and I told you, I must go with my family."

Jesse looked around. "Where's Hotaru?"

"Still at school. She's only months from graduating. She'll be devastated."

Keiko withdrew her hand from Jesse. "You shouldn't be here right now."

"Why not?"

"I must focus on my family. Mother and Roo need me. I'll call you at your office later."

"I'm not going back to the office. Call me at home."

She nodded, then stood. Jesse watched as Keiko walked back to the kitchen, a knot forming in the pit of his stomach.

Was she pulling away already?

Fear gripped him as the sense he could be losing her settled on him like a fog.

MARCH, 1942

The next afternoon, Jesse picked up Keiko as usual, planning to ignore the awkwardness of the night before. He was relieved to find she was back to being herself. They spent their rendezvous as they always did, trying to pack as much as they could into the time they had together, and treasuring every moment. They didn't know when the order to evacuate would come, but they preferred not to talk about it.

Dawn on the last day of March brought the promise of an unseasonably warm afternoon. The forecast called for temperatures near eighty degrees, so Jesse had cooked up a special surprise for Keiko. He'd told her they would be doing something new the next day, and then thwarted her repeated attempts to pry information out of him. Now it was time to deliver.

He picked her up at their usual corner, and she hopped in the vehicle wearing a smile.

"Hey." She kissed him on the cheek. "So, where are we going?"

"Me to know, you to find out. Just sit back and enjoy the drive."

She fixed him with a look of mock anger. "How do I know I'm not being kidnapped?"

"Would it be a problem if you were?"

A sly smile eased its way across her face. "No… I suppose not."

He laughed. "Well then, sit back and behave yourself."

"Okay, I'll be good."

Fifteen minutes later, Jesse stopped the car next to Stow Lake in Golden Gate Park. He pulled up close to the dock where rowboats could be rented.

A huge smile came to her. "Are we going out in a boat?"

"What did I tell you about too many questions?"

"Oh. Sorry, I forgot."

As Keiko climbed out of the car, Jesse reached in the back and retrieved a small basket. He waved at the dock master, then led Keiko down to a waiting boat. He set the basket down, helped her into the boat, and pushed off. Rowing slowly toward the waterfall, Keiko removed her hat and let the sun warm her face.

When he reached a nice spot, Jesse stopped rowing, and let the boat glide. The quiet enveloped them as he reached for the basket. "Are you hungry?"

"A little. What have you got?"

Jesse removed a large package wrapped in a linen towel, and when he unfolded the covering, Keiko squealed. "Are those your mother's oatmeal cookies?"

"They are, and they're still warm."

As Keiko helped herself, Jesse took out a thermos of tea and poured them each a cup. "Mother said to tell you hi."

Keiko finished her third cookie. "Why haven't you introduced me?"

Jesse thought about it. They'd practiced being cautious around her father, but his mother would be happy to meet Keiko. He was foolish for not thinking of it sooner.

"I don't know; I guess 'cause of your dad and always being secretive."

"Do you think she would like me?"

He took her hand. "She'd love you! I'll tell you what; I'm going to fix this grievous oversight on my part. I'll set up a time for us all to be together."

"That sounds like fun."

They sat peacefully for a while, Keiko leaning against his chest, and Jesse couldn't remember a time he was happier. The worry and fear of the war were absent today, their adventure a welcome respite from reality.

****

Her father arrived just a few minutes after Keiko returned to the restaurant. She and Roo were preparing for the dinner rush when a man came to the door. "Is the owner around?"

Keiko pointed to her father's booth. "Back

there."

The man, who Keiko couldn't remember seeing before, went to the last booth. Her father looked up as the man approached and handed him a paper flyer, which her father stared at it while listening to the man explain. When he was finished, the man turned and walked out.

Keiko watched her father, who seemed to be reading the flyer repeatedly from start to finish. Finally, he rose and moved slowly past Keiko to the outside of the restaurant, placing the flyer in the window.

Coming back inside, her father stopped next to her. "It's time, Daughter."

Her stomach dropped, knowing what he meant, but hoping she was wrong. Her father touched her cheek. "I have to tell your mother."

When he walked away, Keiko went and read the flyer for herself. Tears filled her eyes with the first words.

INSTRUCTIONS FOR ALL PEOPLE OF JAPANESE ANCESTRY

A small crowd was beginning to form behind her as she tried to make sense of the notice. It gave a description of the affected area, instructions for where to report, and what to bring. The last line hit Keiko like a bolt of lightning; they were to report on April sixth. One week was all the time they had left.

She went back into the restaurant and found her father sitting in his booth with her mother and Roo. Keiko sat down next to her father, opposite her sister. Both Roo and her mother were crying.

Takeshi was holding his wife's hand. "There's nothing we can do about it. We have one week to get everything done, including the closing of the restaurant, so we'll have to work together. Everyone in the community is in the same boat, so there won't be people to help."

Azumi wiped at her eyes with a napkin. "Where do we start?"

Her father shrugged. "I don't know. I'll go to the JACL and see if they can give us any guidance. The basics are on the notice, but they should have a better idea of the entire process."

Roo sobbed. "What about my schooling? I was supposed to graduate in a couple months."

"You won't be going back. All our energy must be geared toward getting ready."

A family came in, and Keiko looked at her father. "Are we still open?"

"Yes, at least for today. We'll decide the rest after I get back from the community center."

She got up and met the people at the door, seating them near the window. Her mother headed into the kitchen as her father left for the Japanese-American Center. Roo was still sitting quietly when Keiko joined her back at the booth. Her sister's eyes were wide with fear.

"Are you okay, Roo?"

"I'm scared."

"Me too, but Father will take care of us—he always has."

"But where will we go?"

"I don't know. I guess that decision is out of our hands now."

The crowd outside had grown, as had the furor, some people cursing while others cried. The noise fed the panic Keiko was trying to control.

Roo reached across and touched her hand. "Does Jesse know?"

Keiko shrugged. Distracted by the scene around her, she'd forced herself not to think about it, but now the reality of leaving Jesse behind overwhelmed her. It had been there in the back of her mind, almost like a disease she hoped she wouldn't get, but now it had come to pass. They were going to be separated.

Tears ran down her face, and she made no effort to hide them.

As soon as he came in, she spotted him. Their eyes met, and Jesse nodded toward the outside. She bobbed her head slightly, and he returned to the street. It was just a few moments later when she came out onto the sidewalk searching for him.

He waved and she spotted him immediately, ran to him, and wrapped her arms around his neck. Tears stained her face, and tremors shook her body as she clung to him.

After what seemed an eternity, she pulled back, looked over her shoulder, and took his hand. Leading him down the street and behind a grocery store, she guided him to a small bench for people to use on their work breaks.

They sat together, and for a long time, didn't speak.

Keiko laid her head on his shoulder, holding his hand, and running her fingers up and down his arm. Finally, she looked up at him.

"One week! That's all they gave us!"

"I saw that. How will you do it?"

She shrugged. "I have no idea. Father is getting more information now."

"Do you know where they'll send you?"

She shook her head, and looked up at him through teary eyes.

He touched her cheek. "Wherever it is, I'll come see you."

Keiko looked down at her hands. "Will you write?"

"Constantly!"

She laughed, and just for an instant, her world brightened.

He ran his fingers through her hair. "After all, I need to make sure you don't forget me."

"I won't—I can't. I'm going to miss you terribly."

He looked into her in the eyes. "I'll miss

you too. Just promise to take care of yourself. I don't want anything to happen to you."

"I'll be careful."

"Swear?"

"Swear."

****

Her father had still not returned from the JACL Center by evening, and because it was nearly empty, Azumi decided to close the restaurant early. Roo had stayed to help while they did their normal clean up and prep for the next day, but in the back of Keiko's mind, she wondered if *Takeshi's* would ever open again.

When they were done, the three Yoshida women walked the empty streets home. Lights were on in every Japanese residence, people moving about as they worked to get ready, using every moment of the time they had to prepare.

At home, Keiko wanted to do the same, but didn't have a clue where to start. Her mother had planted herself on the couch to wait for Takeshi. Roo was in her room with the door shut, so Keiko went through the kitchen to the backyard. The remnants of the fire were still there, so she pulled up a chair and started poking through them, something she had done many times since that night.

Doves called from a hedge near her—a sad

and haunting coo—appropriate for her mood. What would their new home be like? Would it be warm or cold, and would doves be in the hedges there, too?

The banging of the front door interrupted her thoughts.

Rushing inside, she found her father sitting on the couch next to her mother. A weariness stooped his shoulders and a sadness darkened his face.

Roo came out of her room and joined Keiko across from their parents. Keiko searched his face. "What did you find out, Father?"

He reached into his shirt pocket and retrieved a folded sheet of paper. It was a copy of the notice posted at the restaurant, but scribbled on the back were notes in her father's handwriting. He smoothed it out on the table, took a deep breath, and scanned the three sets of eyes fixed on him.

"I have to go to the assembly center on Bush Street tomorrow, register us, and pick up some documents. On April sixth, we're to report to the center for bussing out of the city."

Keiko's world had become a nightmare. "Is this really going to happen, Father?"

"Some say no, most say yes."

Her mother picked up the note. "What can we bring?"

"Not much, I'm afraid. There's a specific list of what we *must* bring—including linens, cutlery, toiletries, and clothes— but anything else we want to bring, we have to be able to carry."

Azumi turned the paper over, examining her husband's notes. "What about the restaurant?"

"We'll open tomorrow, sell as much of the food as possible, then the next day we'll have a going out of business sale."

"What about our home? What do we do with all our furniture and other belongings?"

"Most of the families are holding 'evacuation sales' in the next few days."

Azumi stared at him. "You mean like a rummage sale?"

Father nodded, and Mother started to cry again.

Keiko sat stunned, watching the exchange between her parents.

This was craziness! Where are all of them supposed to go?

She got up and went to her room. Sitting on her bed, she looked around at her belongings.

What should she bring? Her books? How many could she carry? What should she sell? Does she need warm clothes or should she pack more summer clothes?

It was overwhelming and she wished to talk to Jesse.

Maybe he could help her make sense of it all.

She knew better.

He wouldn't understand the world's current level of insanity any better than she!

Searching again for strength in her mother's words, she said them out loud.

"Shikata ga nai."

The statement may have been true, but it didn't push away the fear that was now her constant companion.

****

The day after the evacuation notices were posted, Jesse was at the office early. Uncle Jerry was already there, and Janet would soon follow. The dominoes had started to fall almost immediately, and the next few days promised to be stress-filled and busy.

Uncle Jerry was on the phone, so Jesse got a cup of coffee and sat down at his desk, his phone lighting up almost immediately. He took a quick sip before picking up the call.

"Sommers Management."

"Jesse Sommers?"

"Yes."

"This is Mr. Kurosawa."

"Good morning, Sir. How can I help you?"

"You have heard the news?"

"About the evacuations? Yes."

"I will be closing my store tomorrow, then

I'll drop my key at your office."

Sadness bore down on Jesse as he realized this was the first of many identical conversations to come. His heart went out to the good people he'd dealt with for years, now forced to shutter their businesses and sell their belongings. He wanted to ask if they would start over when they returned, but the reality was they didn't know *if* they'd return.

"I understand, Mr. Kurosawa. I'm sorry."

"Thank you. Goodbye."

Jesse hesitated in hanging up the phone. Jerry already had another call on hold, and hanging up meant the phone would be ringing again. He finally set the receiver on its cradle, and as expected, it rang immediately.

"Sommers Management."

"Mr. Jesse Sommers?"

"Yes."

"This is Mr. Kato."

And so it went on for the rest of the day. By the time Jesse got away from the office, he was exhausted, but he had an appointment he couldn't miss.

Driving to their normal meeting place, Jesse had to wait nearly thirty minutes, but eventually he spotted her dark hair coming down the crowded sidewalk. Keiko, looking equally tired, got into the car with a weak smile.

"Sorry I'm late. I finally got away by telling Father I wanted to see some old friends for the last time."

"It's no problem. Are you okay?"

"Father just closed down the restaurant for good. It was very hard."

"I'm so sorry, Keiko."

She reached across and took his hand. "You have nothing to be sorry for—it's not your fault."

Jesse forced a smile. "I have a surprise for you."

"Oh? And what would that be?"

"This is one of those situations where you get to sit back and enjoy the ride."

"I see. Well, would it be okay if I scoot over next to you while I enjoy the ride?"

This time he didn't have to force a smile. "I wish you would."

She cuddled against him and he pulled into traffic. When he pulled in the driveway of an unfamiliar suburban home, Keiko sat up, confusion evident on her face. "Where are we?"

He grinned at her. "This is my home."

The house was small, but inviting. A white stucco frame, topped with a green roof, gave the house the feel of a cottage.

"Really? Is your mother home?"

"As a matter of fact, she is. I believe she's fixing some dinner."

"Jesse! How could you?"

Now he was the one confused. "How could I what?"

"Not warn me I was going to meet your mother today."

"Oh," he touched her forehead, brushing back a lock of hair and putting it behind her ear. "You're beautiful—she's going to love you—so don't worry a bit."

Keiko looked toward the front door with apprehension. "I guess…"

"I know. Now, come on. Dinner's ready."

They got out and Jesse took her hand as they walked up the drive. They were almost to the front door, when it suddenly burst open, and his mother stepped out wearing a huge smile.

"Finally!"

Jesse introduced them. "Mom, this is Keiko. Keiko, this is my mother."

Knowing his mother the way he did, Jesse stepped back out of the way. Estelle Sommers danced down the three front steps and wrapped her arms around the surprised girl.

"I'm so glad to finally meet you. Jesse never stops going on about his Keiko."

When Keiko had finally gathered herself, she returned the embrace. "Nice to meet you, Mrs. Sommers."

Estelle stepped back and waved a single finger at her. "Oh, no. Estelle will be just fine. Come in, dinner's ready."

For the next two hours, Jesse was able to forget the events controlling their lives, as Keiko and his mother laughed, told jokes at his expense, and enjoyed each other's company. Near the end of the night, during a lull in the conversation, his mother's expression turned melancholy.

"How is your family coping, Keiko?"

"It's hard. We closed the restaurant today and we'll be having an evacuation sale the day after tomorrow."

Estelle raised an eyebrow. "Evacuation sale?"

"Yes, we have to sell everything."

His mother looked from Keiko to Jesse, then back again. "Everything?"

Keiko nodded.

His mother looked to him for an explanation. "There's a posted list of what they each *must* pack in a single suitcase. Anything else they want to bring has to be carried on their person."

"What about photos, books, heirlooms?"

"If they want them, they have to be carried."

A mixture of anger and sympathy spread across his mother's face. "Keiko, does your family have much they want to keep?"

"Mostly pictures, some mementos from Japan, but we haven't had a chance to sort it all out yet. A lot of the important stuff was burned.
"

"Burned?"

"Yes, anything with Japanese writing on

it, to prevent suspicion of being spies."

Estelle got up, cleared some dishes, and Jesse checked the time. "We need to go, Mom."

She forced a smile and he could tell something was rolling around in her head. "I'm so glad I got to meet you, Keiko."

Keiko stood and started to grab some plates. His mother stopped her. "Don't worry about those; I'll take care of them after you're gone. Give me a hug."

Keiko did, obviously happy to comply. "It was a wonderful meal. Thank you."

"My pleasure. Take care of yourself and we'll see you soon."

"Yes, Mrs. Sommers."

"Tut-tut."

Keiko caught herself. "Yes, Estelle."

"That's better. Jesse, can I have a word with you?"

"Sure."

Jesse stayed behind while Keiko went to the car.

"Jesse, I want you to do something."

"What's that?"

"Tell Keiko to put together a couple boxes of family keepsakes, and on the day of their sale, we'll come by to get them."

"You want to *buy* their family mementos?"

Her look was incredulous. "Of course not! We'll store them here at the house for the family. We don't have much room, but we can take a couple boxes, I'm sure."

Jesse stared at her, then stepped forward to kiss her forehead. "I love you, Estelle Sommers!"

"Tut-tut. You can still call me Mother."

Jesse laughed and headed out to the car. When he got in, Keiko looked at him nervously. "What was that about?"

Jesse told her, and Keiko's eyes filled with tears. "I love your mother. She's so wonderful."

He started the car. "Yeah, well, don't forget it's a package deal. With her, you get me, too."

Keiko pecked him on the cheek. "I wouldn't have it any other way."

****

Keiko spent the next two days preparing to leave. Her father had registered the family at the evacuation center, and when he returned, he carried four white tags. Each tag was hung from a long string, forming a necklace. Roo had picked one up.

"What are these, Father?"

"Identification tags."

"For us?"

"Yes, we each wear one on evacuation day."

"What's the number for?"

Keiko had looked at the tag dangling from her sister's hand. It bore a five-digit stamped number, the family name, their given name, as well as the reporting date and time. They had been identified, selected, and branded. She'd recoiled from them almost instinctively.

Her father retrieved the tag from Roo. "That's our family number. We can be brought back together if we get separated."

They had begun to sell things as April 4 slowly passed. Most of the buyers were merchants looking to pay pennies on the dollar. Keiko tried to ignore what was going on as much as possible. Late in the afternoon, Jesse's car came to a stop behind one of the merchant's trucks.

Keiko watched her father as he walked around the yard with a buyer. They appeared to be bickering on a one-price-for-everything kind of deal. She took advantage of the distraction to fetch the boxes packed with their family treasures. Roo carried one and Keiko the other.

When they reached the car, Jesse already had the back door open, and the boxes quickly disappeared. Jesse closed the door. "See you later?"

Keiko shook her head. "Can't. Nine tomorrow morning, usual place?"

"Okay."

She returned to the sale, and Jesse drove

off.

Block after block, yards were filled with their neighbors' belongings, all going through the same process. Keiko wasn't surprised when her father sold the whole lot to the merchant, figuring he'd seen it was pointless to try to get a decent price for their stuff.

It took over an hour for the man and his companion to load it all up, but when they left, the only things still in the house were the items going with them on their journey. An emptiness surrounded them that echoed the hole inside their hearts.

****

Later that night, Keiko and Roo were called into the kitchen, where their mother waited with a pair of scissors. Keiko pointed at them. "What are those for?"

"We need to cut your hair."

Keiko recoiled. "What? Why?"

"The JACL has recommended it. It is unlikely we will be able to wash and care for your long hair at our destination. It will be easier and more sanitary to cut it short."

"But I don't want to cut it! I want to keep my hair!"

Roo began to cry as their father walked into the kitchen. "Stop it, Roo. It cannot be helped, and there are things more important at stake here."

Roo sniffed, but Keiko turned on her father. "What? What is so important that our personal choice must be sacrificed along with everything else?"

Rather than respond angrily, her father looked away. "It will be safer."

Keiko didn't understand. "Did you say safer?"

"Yes."

"Safer how?"

Her mother answered for him. "You don't want to stand out from the crowd."

Keiko had heard this before. In fact, she'd heard it all her life; it was the honorable thing to conform to society.

But there was more to it for Keiko. Jesse loved her long hair, and she didn't want to lose everything that connected her to him.

"I don't want to conform—I want to be me."

Her father turned back, staring hard at both his daughters.

"You don't want to stand out as a woman in the camps. It could be dangerous."

Keiko was physically rocked backward by her father's suggestion.

Fear rushed to every corner of her being, which Roo apparently could sense.

Recognizing the gravity of the situation, Keiko stepped forward before Roo could start crying again and undid her hair from its bun.

"Very well. I'll go first, Mother."

Twenty minutes later, both girls had hair that barely brushed their shoulders.

****

Keiko was sitting on the corner waiting for Jesse, and stood as he drove up. She climbed into the car, slid over next to him, and removed her hat.

Jesse's surprise was obvious. "Your hair?"

"Mother cut it last night."

"Why?"

"It needed to be short for where we're going."

"Well, I think it's cute."

She didn't believe him. "Yeah, right."

He put his arm around her. "Are you calling me a liar?"

She looked up at him. "You really like it?"

"Sure. It's part of you, and I love you, not your hair."

She leaned up and kissed him, holding it for a long time. The enormity of the moment was not lost on either of them. This would be their last day together.

"Father was not happy about me leaving."

"Did he know where you were going?"

She shook her head. "I don't think so. At

least, if he suspected, he didn't say so."

"What *did* he say?"

"When I said I was going to visit friends, he asked me not to go. He said he was worried about me, but I told him I'd be fine and would see him later. He stared at me for a minute, then nodded."

"Do you think, after all this time, he still doesn't know?"

She shrugged. "I can't say for sure, but I don't know why he would remain silent about it."

Jesse pulled up at Fisherman's Wharf, parked, and got out. He walked around and opened her door, making a flourish by bowing as she got out. "My pleasure to chauffeur you this day, Madam."

Keiko giggled. "Why have you brought me to this place, sir?"

He shut the car door. "I have information that tells me one of your favorite places to eat is located here."

"Do you mean to say you have been checking up on me?"

"No Madam, but I have been speaking with that incredibly handsome man you've been seeing of late."

"Which one?"

He made a face, coaxing another giggle, and poked her side. "I beg your pardon!"

She linked her arm through his. "Lead

away, fine sir."

After lunch, they walked along the pier, ignoring those around them, wrapped in a bubble of their own making. They talked of the day she would return and of what they would rediscover in the weeks after the war, whenever that was.

As the shadows started to grow, he drove them to China Beach and grabbed a blanket from the backseat. Though the day had been warm, it was still early April, and it cooled off as the sun sank in the western sky. They went down by the water and he wrapped it around both of them. "Warm enough?"

"Yes."

"I love you, Keiko Yoshida. Do you know that?"

As a way of saying yes, she snuggled even closer. "I love you too, Jesse Sommers. Do you know that?"

"Swear?"

"Swear."

APRIL 6, 1942

Keiko sat next to her father on the crowded bus, staring out the window. Nothing about the scene around her made sense. Many non-Japanese, who were neighbors and friends, had come to say goodbye. They cried and hugged their friends who were leaving. At the same time, many of those within the Japanese community were smiling and waving, as if they were headed out on holiday.

A procession moved along the side of the bus as bags were loaded and riders filed on. The bus was almost full and the driver was in his seat preparing to leave. A lone soldier stood at the front of the bus, nervously fingering his gun. He looked to be no older than Roo, and clearly wished to be any place but where he found himself.

Keiko sat beside her father and stared out the window. She had hoped to see Jesse, just to know he was there, and to know he was thinking of her. So far, she hadn't been able to pick him out of the crowd. She grew anxious, fighting a rising panic that he'd already forgotten her.

Roo was behind her, sitting next to their mother. A hand reached around the seat and touched her arm.

"Keiko."

She turned to look at her sister, who rolled her eyes toward the front gate. Keiko followed the direction of her sister's gaze.

Standing alone, hands in his pockets and his eyes fixed on her, was Jesse. When she looked his way, he gave her a small wave. Keiko, aware of her father next to her, touched the window with spread fingers. Jesse smiled.

The door on the bus closed with a thump, the engine roared to life, and they slowly pulled away.

Her father leaned toward her, whispering so only she could hear.

"It seems fate has accomplished what my warnings could not."

Keiko spun in her seat to look at him, surprised by his admission. Her father stared straight ahead as the bus passed through the gates.

He'd known all along.

When Keiko looked back at the crowd, Jesse was gone.

She didn't cry—there weren't any tears left—but she did close her eyes. Better to not see her world disappearing.

****

Jesse went inside the bus station, searching the crowd for someone in a War Relocation Authority uniform. He spotted a young man holding a clipboard and trying to answer multiple questions at one time.

Jesse waited his turn, then approached. “Do you know where these buses are going?”

“Woodlands Rail Station.”

“Near Sacramento?”

“That’s the one.”

“Can you tell me where they’ll go from there?”

“Nope.”

“No you can’t, or no you won’t?”

“Look Mister, they only tell us what we need to know, and what I know is the bus goes to the train station at Woodlands.”

“Okay, thanks.”

There was no point in trying to meet Keiko there, so it appeared he would have to wait for her to write before he would know where she had ended up.

****

The bus ride was a little over two hours. They still didn’t know where they were going, just that they would be put on a train, and arrive in a couple days at a temporary home. The mood on the bus had turned sullen, and the trip passed quietly.

Occasionally they would see a banner declaring 'JAPS KEEP MOVING' or a sign announcing 'NO JAPS ALLOWED.'

When the bus finally stopped at the train station, they got off, claimed their suitcases, and formed a line along the platform. Soldiers guarded both ends of the depot.

She heard and felt the approaching train before she saw it.

Pulling into the station with a sinister hiss, it reminded Keiko of a giant snake arriving to draw them into its coils, and she retreated instinctively. With one last giant gasp, the train ceased all motion.

Small portable steps were put down for people to climb onto the train. Several of the old Pullman coaches were already full, but the window shades were drawn, so you couldn't make out who was inside.

After they were seated in their car, and the train had begun to move out of the station, the soldiers walked the aisle. Two of them were stationed in each car, and they ordered the shades be pulled down until they were out of Sacramento. This instruction was repeated every time they went through a new town, but Keiko never learned why.

Frequently stopping to take on more people, they traveled for two days. Keiko and Roo passed the time by reading, playing cards, or sleeping. Every time a civilian train came from the opposite direction, they were set off to the side to wait its passing, then allowed to go on their way.

By the end of the second day, Keiko had become uncomfortably anxious about where they were headed. One of the soldiers came by, moving slowly to his post at the far end of the car, when Keiko touched his arm. The young man turned quickly, pointing his weapon. She recoiled in fear, but when she looked into his eyes, she was surprised.

He appeared more afraid than her.

"I'm sorry, I didn't mean to…"

He returned his weapon to his side. "It's okay. What is it?"

"Do you know where we're going?"

"Santa Anita Assembly Center."

Keiko wasn't familiar with Santa Anita, and the confusion must have shown on her face.

The young soldier smiled slightly. "It's near Los Angeles."

"Oh…thanks."

"You're welcome."

He continued to the front of the car, and Keiko turned to her mother.

"We're going to Los Angeles. An Assembly Center called Santa Anita."

Her mother tried to smile. "I'm sure it will be very nice."

Keiko was quite sure her mother was

wrong.

****

The next morning, as Keiko was just waking, the train began to slow. When she looked out the window, the skyline of Los Angeles filled the distant horizon, before being quickly blocked by the station they were pulling into. A sign above the platform declared they'd arrived in Arcadia, California.

Within an hour, they'd been off-loaded from the train, delivered to the Santa Anita Assembly Center, and were standing in line to be processed. The crush of humanity around Keiko stole her breath. Their bodies were pressed one against another as they were moved from one line to the next. She distracted herself by focusing on keeping Roo from getting lost.

The first line was to get inoculated. She wasn't sure what was in the needle, but everyone going into the camp had to have the shot, and it wasn't until all four of them were done that they could get in the next line, which turned out to be for their quarters.

Santa Anita Racetrack had been given to the war relocation effort, and the internees were housed in converted stables. Their new home was a horse stall with a single light bulb hanging from the ceiling. They each had a cot, a blanket, and a mattress stuffed with straw.

The walls were eight feet high, but didn't extend to the ceiling, meaning they could hear everything going on in the other stalls. Her mother struggled with the lack of privacy, and Father seemed weighed down with shame. Roo cried most of the time, so Keiko would sit next to her on the cot and hold her.

As Keiko had suspected, her mother was wrong. This place was not a 'nice place' at all. In fact, it was miserable.

The only bright spot was visitation, which Keiko quickly learned was available to people outside the camps, and she sent a letter to Jesse as soon as she could. After that, there was nothing to do but stand in more lines. Each day spent waiting for showers, for food, and worst of all, for the toilets.

****

Keiko looked along the line of people's heads in front of her, a snake of field hats that stretched over two hundred yards. Her father had made a habit of standing in line for the mail, something he insisted he only should do, but he had a meeting this day. Keiko volunteered to take his place and her father had reluctantly agreed. She almost changed her mind and opted to let her father come the next day.

A letter from Jesse was the only reason she'd volunteered, and though she didn't know if one would be waiting, neither did she want to wait until the next day to find out. Three hours later, her patience paid off when the postmaster laid a yellow envelope in her hand, the familiar handwriting sending a charge through her.

Moving out into the sun where she could sit on the grass infield of the track, she opened the envelope. Her head started to spin slightly and she had to remind herself to breathe.

My Dear Keiko,

I miss you so much, and was very excited to get your letter this morning. It's now evening, and I'm in my room, trying to think of all the things I want to say.

I'm sorry to hear about your living conditions. It saddens me to think about what you and your family are going through. While the war is making life difficult for all, at least I am in my own bed, and not having my choices controlled by others. When I think about it, I get so angry, but it does me no good.

At the same time, I can understand people's fear after Pearl, and why they're making the decisions they are. I wish so much that you didn't have to pay the price for something you didn't support or condone.

On a lighter note, I have made enquiries

about coming to visit you, but don't have a firm date yet. Uncle Jerry said I can have whatever time off I need. He has been very good to Mother and I.

Speaking of Mother, she wants you to know she is praying for you every day, as am I. Say hi to Roo and Azumi for me. I don't know how long we'll be apart, but until that day, you are constantly in my thoughts.

Hope to see you soon,
Love, Jesse

She read it again, wiping at her eyes with the sleeve of her shirt, and then put it away. Walking back to her room, she did her best to focus on his upcoming visit, and not let the pain in her heart get control.

Roo looked up when Keiko came in. "Judging by your eyes, I'd say there was no letter."

"Actually, there was."

"That's great! Why the red eyes? Did he break it off with you?"

Keiko dropped down next to her sister. "No. I just miss him so much."

"Can I read it?"

Keiko gave Roo the letter and waited.

Roo handed it back. "Did you tell him I said hi?"

Keiko nodded.

Roo sighed. "You're so lucky."

"What do you mean?"

"I don't have a sweet guy missing me!"

Keiko thought about it, then smiled. "Yeah, I guess I am."

****

It had been two full weeks since Jesse had started calling for an appointment at Santa Anita. He called all day long, dialing every thirty minutes, but the line was always busy. Finally, when someone did answer, he almost missed it daydreaming.

"Santa Anita Assembly Center."

"Oh…yes, my name is Jesse Sommers and I would like to make a visitation appointment."

The female voice was all business. "Family name and number?"

"Yoshida, 16573."

There was a long pause followed by the sound of flipping pages. "I have an opening a week from Thursday."

Jesse's heart sunk. "That's two weeks from now, is there nothing sooner?"

"I'm sorry, sir. We're jammed up. It's at three o'clock, do you want it or not?"

"Yes…yes, thank you."

"What did you say your name was?"

"Jesse Sommers."

"Very well, you're scheduled and the family will be notified."

Before Jesse could thank her, the phone went dead. He hung up and dashed a letter off to Keiko with the details of the visit. When he finished, he went to the calendar on the wall, wrote the appointment down, then stared at it.

Keiko will have been gone nearly two months before he would finally get to see her.

He mumbled to himself. "Shikata ga nai."

"What was that?"

Jesse turned to see Janet watching him. "Oh nothing, just a saying Keiko taught me."

MAY, 1942

The drive down to Arcadia, California, was easily eight hours, and Jesse planned to drive straight through, spending the night near Santa Anita. Eventually, he had to admit he was having trouble staying awake, and pulled off near Bakersfield to get some sleep. He would have a little over two hours left to drive the next morning.

He slept in, caught a light breakfast, then hit the road. Arriving at the Assembly Center just past one o'clock in the afternoon, he was greeted by a sight that was both amazing and shocking.

Chain link fence, topped with barbed wire, surrounded the several hundred acres of Santa Anita Racetrack, including the grandstand, stables, and the pastures behind the facility. Every few hundred yards was a tall wooden guard tower, manned by soldiers with rifles on their shoulders, and using binoculars to watch the movement inside the fence.

The fields had been overrun by barracks, some five hundred buildings in all, row upon row stretching into the distance from where he stood. The size and scope of the camp was intimidating. After parking, he joined hundreds of others in a line at the front of the visitors' door.

At two-forty-five, he finally reached the front of the line, where he was greeted by a young soldier at a table, who didn't look up when Jesse approached. "What is the family name you're visiting?"

"Yoshida."

"Identification number?"

"16573."

The soldier scanned the papers in front of him, made a mark next to one of the columns, then finally looked up at Jesse. "Your name?"

"Jesse Sommers."

"ID?"

Jesse handed him his driver's license. The soldier studied it, wrote down the number, then handed it back. "You're clear to proceed. Go to table 274 and wait for the person your meeting."

Jesse took the license and looked toward the set of doors behind the soldier. "Through there?"

"Yes."

When Jesse opened the doors, he was struck by a tidal wave of noise. The large cafeteria-like setting was filled with people conversing and hugging; many were crying. The noise level was slightly disorientating, and it took him a minute to get his bearings, but eventually he found the table numbered 274.

There was another family at the table, and they took up most of the seating, but Jesse sat on the end while he searched for Keiko in the crowds of people milling about. It appeared most camp residents were coming and going through a large set of double doors at the back of the room.

Jesse scanned each new arrival for the familiar face he'd missed so much, his heart pounding with anticipation built up over the past two months. What he eventually saw sent a chill through him. Appearing at the door, speaking to a soldier, and them moving in Jesse's direction was Takeshi Yoshida. There was no sign of Keiko behind him.

Jesse stood as Keiko's father drew closer, and extended his hand. Mr. Yoshida nodded instead, and sat down.

Jesse lowered himself down opposite the man. "Mr. Yoshida, I didn't expect to see you today."

"I don't imagine you did."

Jesse looked hopefully toward the double doors. "Is Keiko coming also?"

Takeshi shook his head. "Keiko is very ill and on bed rest."

Jesse's heart pounded. "What's wrong?"

"Dysentery. It has made her very weak."

"Will she be okay?"

"If we can keep enough fluids in her. It's pretty bad."

Jesse's shoulders sagged. "Is there any way I can see her?"

"I am afraid not."

Jesse stood to leave.

"Jesse, please sit."

Jesse considered ignoring the request.

Takeshi pointed at the seat. "Please. There is more to discuss."

Jesse relented, sitting and staring at Takeshi, waiting.

Takeshi met his gaze. "You know how I feel about you and my daughter, correct?"

Jesse nodded.

"And you assume it's because you are not Japanese, right?"

Jesse shrugged, but didn't answer.

Takeshi leaned closer. "It is true that I would *prefer* Keiko marry a Japanese boy, but that is only part of the reason I stand against your relationship."

Takeshi hesitated, and Jesse watched as the man searched for words.

Finally, Takeshi gestured at the scene around them. "Look at this room, Jesse. What do you see?"

Jesse did as he was asked. "Folks visiting the people who have been interned."

"And what nationality are the interned."

"Japanese."

"And what nationality are most of the visitors?"

Jesse scanned the room, seeing for the first time that he was in the minority.

"The same."

"Do you know what many of the conversations are about?"

"No, sir."

"They're discussing what it is like to be interned. Those who have not been incarcerated yet want to know so they can try to prepare their own family."

Jesse swallowed hard as Takeshi's eyes now bored into his.

"This room, these people, our captivity—they are Keiko's war. You are on the other side of the fence, and you cannot begin to understand the flame by which she is being seared."

There was no anger in his voice, but Jesse could sense bitterness. Jesse was desperate. "But I love your daughter, Mr. Yoshida."

"Do you?"

"Yes…"

"Then let her alone. Let her use what strength she has to fight her daily battle to survive."

"But…"

"None of us knows how long this will continue," Takeshi was now only inches from Jesse's face. "But the war you find yourself in is different than hers. Let Keiko focus on her fight and you move forward with your own."

Jesse's heart ached. The noise around him

had disappeared. His world was filled with despair.

Takeshi stood. "I must go now, but please think about what I've said. It is for the best."

As the man walked away, Jesse could find no words to stop him.

He didn't agree with Takeshi, but he couldn't deny his truth.

****

Jesse returned home late Friday afternoon. When he came into the house, he found his mother on the couch with a blanket, listening to the war news on the radio. He hadn't wanted to worry her, so when he called her, he'd deflected questions about the visit.

He kissed her on the forehead, and she patted the couch next to her. "Sit. Tell me all about your visit with Keiko."

Jesse dropped his suitcase at the kitchen door, before returning to the couch. He started with a description of the camp, then the waiting in line, and finally, the conversation with Takeshi.

She was silent until he was finished, then appeared to be weighing her response. "What did you tell him?"

"You mean did I agree to leave her alone?"

"Exactly."

"I didn't say either way. He asked me to think about it."

"Do you think she was *really* sick?"

"I don't know. The same thought crossed my mind, but I don't suppose it matters. His request remains the same either way."

After sitting together quietly for nearly an hour, Jesse stood. "What do you think I should do?"

"I'm not sure, Jesse, but I know this; whatever you decide, it will be the right choice."

He gave her a weary smile. "Thanks, Mom. Goodnight."

AUGUST, 1942

Letters had continued to arrive from Keiko in the months since Jesse's visit. In each case, she asked why he hadn't come down to see her and why he wasn't writing. Jesse now understood what was happening; Takeshi was intercepting the letters he mailed and keeping his daughter in the dark.

When he received an envelope that bore her handwriting, he would feverishly open it, only to have the pain in her words tear at his soul. He wanted to find a way to see her, to get to her without Takeshi knowing, but he couldn't get approval for another visit.

His feelings for Keiko were too strong to walk away from, and his frustration had reached a crescendo with the news Santa Anita would be closing soon. All internees would be moved to their permanent camps.

Keiko had mentioned an illness among the internees , and Jesse continued to worry about her. He sat at the kitchen table re-reading the latest letter, sensing she was giving up on ever seeing him again. His mother came into the kitchen, got a drink of water, and sat down across from him.

"Another letter from Keiko?"

He nodded. "There has to be a way to get in touch with her."

"You'll think of something."

"I've been racking my brain for weeks."

She sipped her water. "What about her sister?"

"Hotaru? What about her?"

"Maybe Mr. Yoshida is not monitoring *her* mail."

Jesse smacked his forehead so hard his head jerked backward.

"Of course! Why didn't I think of that?"

He jumped up from the table, went to his bedroom, and returned with an envelope.

"Will you write the address for me? Your handwriting might help disguise who the letter is from."

"Be glad to. How do you spell her name?"

Jesse fed his mother all the information, then turned to writing his letter.

My Dear Keiko,

I hope this letter finds its way to you. I have received every letter you've sent and answered each one in turn, but you are not getting them. I can only assume your father is trying to keep us apart, as he told me on my visit to the camp.

That's correct, I came to visit you, but your father said you were ill. He asked me to let you be, but I can't and won't. I love you too much.

Don't be too angry with Takeshi. He's only doing what he thinks is best for you, but know that my feelings for you have never changed.

I've heard the camp will be closing soon and you'll be moving to a place even farther away. I can only hope this awful war will be over soon and you can come home to me.

Missing you,
Love, Jesse

He folded the note up and put inside an envelope, wrote *Keiko* on it, then slipped it inside the envelope his mother had addressed to Roo. He would mail it the next morning at work, and pray that this time it would land in Keiko's hands.

****

Keiko sat in the train car, just months after arriving at Santa Anita, and stared out at the passing mountains. Their grandeur was undeniable, but she didn't care, they were just the landscape along the way to another camp. This one was known as Heart Mountain.

Santa Anita hadn't been a pleasant

experience, but at least it was warm; even she knew northern Wyoming was going to be desperately cold during the winter.

Roo lay against her, sleeping. Her younger sister had lost some of her zeal in their time at the assembly center, and Keiko worried Roo was becoming despondent; even her high school graduation ceremony hadn't lightened her mood.

Reaching into her pocket, Keiko pulled out the only letter she'd received from Jesse since the day she left San Francisco. Worn and beginning to fray around the edges from frequent handling, she read it daily, searching for some hidden indication of why he hadn't written again. There was nothing, and the not knowing constantly ate at her, slowly stealing the little hope she still had.

The train came down from the mountains and moved onto a long, flat plain. Within a few hours, they slowed in front of a huge compound, nestled near the base of a snow-capped peak. Barbed wire stretched as far as she could see, and uniformed soldiers manned gun towers around the perimeter.

Long rows of barracks, little more than wood buildings covered with tarpaper, ran away from the camp entrance to somewhere in the distance. The aura of this camp was much more like a prison than Santa Anita.

When her family stepped off the train,

they were confronted by soldiers pointing and giving orders. Their baggage had preceded them, and was lying in a huge pile just inside the gate. Each family searched through it until they found their belongings, then fell in line to begin registration. After being checked into the camp, they were directed toward the barrack that was to be their new home.

Roo remained silent, staying close to Keiko's side and looking directly at the ground in front of her, as their father led the way. Their mother walked behind them, making sure they didn't get separated.

After struggling for nearly half a mile over the hard, uneven ground, their father turned toward one of the long barrack buildings, and forced a smile. "This is it. Wait here."

Takeshi crossed a wooden plank bridge leading over a gulley of mud.

Keiko, Roo, and their mother stood in the chilly autumn wind, waiting for Takeshi to reemerge from the building. After several minutes, he came back outside, this time without his luggage. He crossed the little bridge to where they stood, forced another smile, then took Azumi's bag. "We're at the far end."

He turned and headed back inside, this time followed by his family. It took a minute for Keiko's eyes to adjust, but when they did, her new world came as a shock.

The long structure was divided into rooms

on either side of a long hallway that ran the length of the building. Some smaller ones appeared to be for individuals, and the larger ones for families.

At the far end, they turned into a room with four cots, each loaded with two blankets. In the center was a cast-iron, pot-bellied stove. A single bare light bulb hung from the ceiling above.

Keiko stood there, not quite sure what to do next. Her father started giving directions, but Keiko wasn't listening.

Finally, he touched her shoulder. "Keiko?"

She blinked. "Yes?"

"You take the cot next to Hotaru."

She looked over at her sister, who was sitting on a cot by the wall, her legs drawn up under her chin. Keiko forced herself forward, setting her bag on the floor, and sitting on her own cot. The noise of other families locating their own quarters came to her through the walls. As the building began to fill, it became loud to the point of overwhelming, and she found herself covering her ears.

There was no other furniture at all. No table, chairs, closets, or benches. Just exposed exterior walls made of two-by-fours and covered by tarpaper. Keiko wasn't sure it was any warmer inside the building than outside.

Roo was staring at the wall next to her bed. "I can see outside."

Her father walked over to look. "Yeah, we'll have to do something about that."

Keiko peered at the wall by her. It was the same, and a look at the floor revealed gaps between the planks there also. "Why are there so many holes, Father?"

"I imagine they built these barracks pretty quickly, which means they used green wood. It is shrinking as it dries. Perhaps we can scrounge up something to plug some of them."

Her mother stood. "Do either of you girls need to use the bathroom?"

They both did.

"Okay, let's see if we can find the facilities."

As they headed down the hallway, Takeshi caught up with them. "I'm going to find us some coal for the stove."

Azumi nodded. "We'll see you back here."

Each block of barracks had its own toilet building, shower house, and dining hall. The three Yoshida women followed the signs and came around a corner to find a long line, entirely made up of women and girls. The sign over the door read 'Ladies Toilet,' and a constant flow of women moved in and out. Keiko and Roo followed their mother to the back of the line.

Roo nudged her sister. "Do you smell that?"

Keiko nodded. "I smelled it before we

ever came around the corner."

"It's disgusting!"

"Looks like they didn't build enough toilets."

The line moved slowly forward, and as the entrance came into view, Keiko watched the horror spread across her mother's face.

Azumi Yoshida, like most Japanese women of her generation, was extremely private. The bathroom she was faced with using was unlike anything she'd experienced before, and Keiko sensed her mother was on the verge of tears.

Moving out of the sun and into the building, they were met by a sight they were unprepared for, and barely able to comprehend. Long sinks lined the exterior walls, apparently for hand washing, but there was no soap. The women coming out of the bathroom had rinsed their hands and were shaking them dry as they left.

Down the middle of the room ran six toilets side-by-side, and backing up against six others, with no dividers or screens between the individual stalls.

By the time they exited the building, Keiko was close to vomiting, and her mother *had* started crying.

When the Yoshida women returned to the room, Takeshi had a small fire going in the cast-iron stove. Keiko couldn't tell any difference in the temperature, but the orange glow made her feel a little better.

Her stomach growled. "What do we do about food?"

Her father turned from stoking the fire. "We're scheduled to eat in an hour."

"Scheduled?"

"Yes. The dining hall can't hold everyone in our block at the same time, so we eat in shifts, and ours is the third shift."

The sun was going down, and a gust of wind forced the frigid night air through the floor cracks, making Keiko retreat to her cot and blankets. The family sat quietly, each lost in their own thoughts, waiting for their turn to eat. Finally, her father stood. "Put your heavy coats on. It's time to go."

As they approached the dining hall, a now familiar site greeted them. Another long line stretched out from the cafeteria entrance. They joined the procession and Roo snuggled up against Keiko, trying to keep warm.

When they did get inside, Keiko suspected any warmth was the result of all the people jammed in the building, rather than real heat. Still, it was better than standing in the wind.

Dinner was Vienna sausages, string beans, and rice. If she hadn't been so hungry, she would have refused it. She gave herself a fifty-fifty chance of keeping it down.

Roo was chewing and making faces at the

same time, prompting Keiko to laugh. "Isn't it yummy, Roo?"

"I don't know; I'm doing my best to swallow without tasting."

Keiko giggled, probably from exhaustion as much as anything. "That would explain all the funny faces you're making!"

Roo started to giggle as well, spewing a small amount of green bean and rice mixture onto the table, and soon they were laughing. It was rejuvenating to smile, despite the difficult circumstances, and soon their mother was smiling along with them.

The good humor lasted until they returned to their room, at which point the girls climbed into bed. Keiko lay there bundled up, her jacket still on, and pictured Jesse.

She prayed he was in a better situation than she was, and she hoped he hadn't forgotten about her.

The vision of his smile allowed her to escape her surroundings, and eventually, to fall asleep.

JANUARY, 1943

Life had fallen into a routine for the Yoshidas and the rest of the internees at Heart Mountain. Roo was working as an assistant schoolteacher, Azumi worked in the kitchen, and Takeshi was sorting mail in the camp post office. Keiko had found a job as a receptionist at the camp hospital. The time she spent working helped to distract her from the harsh conditions.

Winter in Wyoming was colder than Keiko ever dreamed possible, and efforts to stay warm were a never-ending struggle. Both Christmas and New Year's had passed without much fanfare. A few carols sung in the dining hall, or an occasional 'Happy New Year' greeting to a passerby were the only signs of the season.

Roo stopped by on her way home from work each day to pick up Keiko, and they would walk together to the barracks. Keiko would immediately check to see if her father had brought home a letter from Jesse. So far, not a word and it had been nearly six months since the only letter she'd received.

The family's room was now divided in half by a hanging blanket, and the girls slept on one side, while their parents slept on the other.

The only form of seating was a couple of old fruit crates their father had scrounged up.

Early in January, Keiko and Roo arrived home to hear their parents arguing. Their father's voice rising as they approached. "It's for the best, Azumi."

"I'm not sure we're doing the right thing."

"It's the only way, and it must be done. Now, let me have it."

There was a brief hesitation before their mother answered. "Very well."

Takeshi came barging through the hanging blanket, nearly toppling Roo, before marching down the center of the barracks.

Keiko went into where her mother sat staring down at her hands. "Mother?"

Azumi jumped. "Oh, Keiko. I didn't know you were home. Is Hotaru with you?"

"Yes. Why was father angry?"

Her mother's eyes shifted away. "It's nothing."

"Are you okay?"

"Yes dear, I'm fine."

Keiko knew better than to push her mother, and changed the subject. "How was work?"

"Busy. I got a raise today."

"Really? That's great."

"Yeah, and now I'm the highest paid cook on my shift."

Nobody in the camp made much at their

jobs, since an Army Private fighting on frontlines only made twenty-one dollars a month, and internees weren't allowed to make more than a soldier.

Still, a raise was a raise. "I'm proud of you, Mother."

"Thank you, Daughter."

****

It was a couple weeks later, when Keiko and Roo were walking home, that Roo brought up the subject of Jesse. "You still haven't heard from him?"

Keiko shook her head. "Not since the letter at Santa Anita."

"Have you written him?"

"Several times. I'm afraid he may have decided to move on."

Roo jumped in front of her, blocking her sister's progress. "I don't believe that! Jesse loves you."

Keiko stood staring into her sister's eyes, wanting to agree, wanting to believe with the same confidence, but she couldn't muster the hope. "I'm not so sure, Roo."

"Well, I am—you'll see."

"Hey, Hotaru!"

Both girls turned to see who had called out. Roo spotted him and grabbed Keiko's arm, restarting their walk home. "Ignore him and keep moving."

"Who is he?"

"His name is Dennis Coleman. His father is the Camp Administrator."

He was catching up to them. "Aren't you going to say hi? I know you like me."

Roo scowled and turned to face the boy. "Leave me alone, Dennis."

"Oh, come on. How about the dance next week? You and me."

The camp had started holding a few social activities, including dances, and the one celebrating Valentine's Day was coming up.

Keiko studied the young man. He was tall, nearly six feet, with sandy brown hair, and gangly features. He wasn't unattractive, but his personality seemed to be ugly. Roo resumed their walk, picking up the pace. "I'm not going to a dance or anywhere else with you. Now, get lost."

"Hotaru, we're meant for each other. Let me take you—it'll be fun."

Keiko had heard enough. She spun quickly, meeting the young man's stare. "It sounds to me like she's made herself perfectly clear."

Dennis stopped short and smirked at Keiko, running his gaze from her head to feet, and back again. "You must be Keiko?"

"And you are rude!"

"Hey, I just want to get to know your sister a little better."

Keiko stepped closer, her face now just inches from his. "Leave her alone. Am I being clear?"

"Or what?"

"I'll report you."

Dennis laughed. "To who, my father?"

Keiko turned and took Roo by the arm. "Let's go. We're wasting our time here."

As they walked off, Dennis called after them. "Nice talking to you. See you tomorrow, Hotaru."

When they were well clear of him, Keiko slowed down. "How long has he been bothering you?"

Roo shrugged. "A few weeks, I guess."

"Why didn't you tell me?"

"It didn't seem to be a big deal at the time. We just said hi a couple times, but now he won't stop bugging me."

"Can you avoid him on the way home from work?"

"Not really. He shows up before I'm done."

Keiko wasn't going to tolerate her sister being harassed. "From now on, I'll come pick *you* up. You wait at work for me to get there."

"That's not necessary…"

"Promise you'll wait for me."

"But…"

"Promise!"

"Fine, but it's not necessary..."

"Don't care—you just promised."

Roo stared at her, trying to look annoyed, but Keiko could see the relief in her sister's eyes.

There was more to the situation than Roo was telling her—she could feel it. He scares her sister, and Roo wasn't one who got scared easily.

****

Valentine's Day was just around the corner, and Jesse had hoped for a response to his latest letter by now, but he had to admit he wasn't completely surprised that nothing had arrived. Whatever was keeping Keiko from writing, he couldn't do much about it.

His mother was at a ladies' church function on the day he arrived home to find a letter in the box with a postmark from Wyoming.

His heart thumped in his ears as he grabbed the letter and hurried inside. Dropping onto the couch, and carefully opened the thick envelope.

In a heart stopping instant, he recognized a second envelope tucked inside. It was his own letter.

He pulled it out and turned it over. Attached to the back was a note in a woman's handwriting.

Mr. Sommers,

I am sorry to inform you of the passing of my daughter, Keiko. The illness finally took her from us.

Regretfully,

Azumi Yoshida.

Jesse stared at the writing, not really seeing, not really understanding.

He read it again.

No…no…no! It couldn't be.

He dropped the letter on the floor and slid off the couch to his knees.

An agony inside flowed through him, as if his own blood was carrying the pain to the deepest reaches of his being.

Everything he had been living for was founded in his love for Keiko. Now, nothing remained of the future he'd pictured, fought for, and believed in.

He folded the letter to his chest and rolled on his side, curling into a fetal position.

Deep sadness took over his world.

****

Sometime later, Jesse felt himself being shaken.

"Jesse? Jesse!"

He stirred, trying to gather himself, not sure where he was.

"Oh, thank the dear Lord! I thought you were dead."

He sat up. "Mom?"

"Are you okay, Son?"

It came surging back. The letter, the pain, the despair. He looked down at the floor and picked up the envelope, handing it to his mother. As she read, he pushed himself back up onto the couch.

"Oh, no. Oh, Jesse, I'm so sorry."

She sat next to him, putting her arm around his shoulders, and wiped at her own tears. They sat that way for a long while, just rocking each other in silence. Eventually, Estelle got up and retrieved some tissue.

"Here."

Jesse accepted the wad she handed him, not using it, instead turning it over and over in his hands. "I don't know what to do now. We had the rest of our lives planned—beginning with the day this stupid war was over."

She sat in a chair across from him. "I've been there, Jesse—when your father died."

"How did you make it?"

"In the beginning, I couldn't look beyond the next hour. Eventually, I could look ahead to the next day. And after a very long time, I was able to look at the future in terms of months and years."

"I can't even face tonight. Where did you find the strength?"

"From you."

Jesse looked up, his brows knit together. "Me?"

She nodded. "You. I had to go on for you. I had to be there for you."

He managed a weak smile. "And you *were* there, always."

Her eyes met his gaze. "You have to find what it is that gives you a reason to continue. You may not see it today, tomorrow, or even for months. But this much I know—you *will* find it."

****

The calendar had turned over to May before Jesse got the courage to visit the one place he could say goodbye. He parked the sedan next to the seawall and stared out at the steady arrival of the waves, his own emotions washing over him in a similar way, as if he was the beach.

Finally, he forced himself to get out and walk slowly down the concrete steps. China Beach was empty, except for the resident gulls.

Their silly walk reminded him of Keiko and her laugh.

He took his shoes off and left them by the stairs. He wanted the sand he and Keiko had curled up on many times to be pushed up through his toes. Her surprise at the hidden beach, and the privacy they'd had there, were still fresh in his mind.

This was it. The place where it all started for them. He never imagined it would end up being a place of pain.

His foot kicked up a sand dollar from the sand. Instead of reaching for it, he pulled from his pocket the shell Keiko had left for him at the hospital. He caressed it, remembering the delight on her face when she'd first found it.

Walking to the edge of the water, he let the waves roll over his feet. Staring out at the bay, the late afternoon sun was reflected off the water and played across his face.

The shell was the last thing he had of her. The heavens had claimed her, and so now he had no choice but to let her go.

With sudden impulse and force of will, he kissed the shell, reared back, and threw it as far as he could.

Tears blurred his vision as he lifted his face toward the sky.

"Goodbye, my dear Keiko."

SPRING, 1943

Spring in the camp was a time to refresh from the rigors of winter. The men and women who had come from a farming background, with the blessing of the camp administrator, had turned one corner of the huge compound into a vegetable garden. Heart Mountains, now nearly full, had become organized with classes, sports leagues, and social clubs.

"Are you going with me?"

Keiko looked at her sister, who standing at the door with a towel over her shoulder. A swim sounded good.

"I really should finish this my sewing…"

"The water is nice and cool."

"Oh, alright! Wait for me outside."

Roo giggled. "I knew you'd give in."

Swimming was one of their favorite things to do, especially during the heat of the day. Keiko caught up with Roo, and they made their way to the swimming hole. As usual, it was crowded and several of their friends were already there.

Roo dropped her towel and took off running. "Last one in is a loser!"

Keiko dropped her own towel and ran after

her, catching her just before the water, and pushing Roo aside. She propelled herself out over the water and, as she was about to splash down, someone surfaced right in front of her. She landed on their back, pushing them under.

When both of them popped up, Keiko immediately apologized. "I'm so sorry. Are you okay?"

The young man turned toward her, a big smile on his face. "I'm fine. If you wanted to say hi, you didn't have to jump on me."

Despite the cool water, Keiko's face flushed red. "No…I mean…it was an accident."

He feigned disappointment. "Aww, you mean you didn't want to meet me?"

"Well, no…yes."

He laughed. "Which is it?"

Keiko tried to gather herself. "I'm Keiko."

He tipped his head toward her. "I am Shoji. Pleased to meet you."

Roo had stopped on the bank. "Are you okay, Sis?"

Keiko waved at her. "Fine."

When she turned around, Shoji was gone. She searched out across the swimming hole but didn't see him surface.

"Look out!"

A giant splash momentarily blinded Keiko. When her vision cleared, he was standing there grinning at her. "Got you back."

She laughed. "I suppose we're even then."

"I suppose so."

He was taller than her, with longer hair than most of the boys, and a laugh that instantly cheered her. They floated and talked for nearly an hour until he said he had to go.

"See you here again, Keiko?"

She smiled. "I think that's likely."

"Just come up and say hi next time, okay?"

"No promises."

Later, in bed and dozing off, she thought of Jesse for the first time that day. It surprised her, and struck her as a little sad.

Had she given up? Should she let him go?

Suddenly, neither sleep nor answers came easy.

****

With the end of June came the heat of July and August, and the ability to escape the oppression was limited to the occasional thunderstorm and trips to the swimming hole. Keiko, Roo, and several of the other girls, made the trek out to the cool water every day after work.

Keiko had more than one reason for going, and it had become the highlight of her day, when she had a chance to see Shoji. He was friendly, warm, and funny; all of which made camp life easier to take.

On this late afternoon, he was absent, and after swimming for over an hour, they called it a day. Keiko toweled off and headed for home, assuming Roo was right behind her. She was more than fifty yards down the trail when she heard a commotion. Turning around, she spotted Roo in a shouting match with a boy.

Dennis!

Keiko ran back toward the argument, arriving as Roo pushed Dennis backwards. "Don't touch me!"

Dennis came back at her, his smirk transforming to anger. "Don't push me, you Jap!"

Keiko stepped between the two, her glare freezing the startled Dennis. "That's enough!"

Dennis hesitated, apparently intimidated by the older Keiko, then pointed at Roo. "We're not through!"

He bent over and snatched up his towel, before walking over to where his friends stood.

Keiko looked at Roo. "Are you okay?"

"Fine! He's a jerk."

They started for home, this time with Keiko staying behind her sister. "What happened?"

Roo looked over her shoulder at the retreating group of boys before answering.

"He asked me to go to the Fourth of July dance and I told him no. He tried to put his arm around me, but I pushed him away."

"I thought he was old news."

"He is. I don't see him much, but occasionally we cross paths, and he starts up again."

"Starts up how?"

"Oh, you know. He says how he still likes me, still thinks about me—stuff like that."

Keiko opened the door to the barracks. "Has he ever touched you before?"

"No..."

Keiko sensed the hesitation. She shut the door and faced her sister.

"Roo, has he ever touched you before? Don't lie to me."

"Just once. He took my hand and tried to kiss it, but I pulled away."

Keiko forced Roo to meet her gaze. "Roo, listen to me. That is not okay, and you have to tell me if it happens again. Understand?"

"I'm not afraid of him."

"I don't care if you're afraid or not—you have to tell me!"

"Okay, okay. I promise."

****

Jesse found the summer of 1943 difficult. Business was still slow, and he had a lot of time on his hands, so he'd taken to going down by the Golden Gate Bridge. As he did on this evening, he'd walk out on the span, taking in the view and feeling the breeze. It brought him a sense of peace.

Sometimes, he'd pass other regulars that seemed to be on the same mission. They'd tip hats, say hi, and keep going. He'd stop and lean against the rail, looking out toward the harbor mouth, and think of the fighting men out across that huge expanse of the Pacific Ocean.

He'd given up feeling bitter about not being able to go. *Shikata ga nai* had become his personal mantra, helping him deal with the war, Keiko's death, and the other struggles of daily life. It was obvious to all that, until the war was over, nothing would truly change.

He looked at his watch, took a last glance at the setting sun, then turned toward where his car was parked. As he walked along, he spotted a figure roughly twenty yards ahead of him, standing outside the railing. The man, about Jesse's age, was gripping the rail with both hands behind him. His eyes were closed, and as Jesse got closer, he could see the man was crying.

As soon as he was within earshot, as calmly as he could, Jesse called out. "Hey, friend!"

The man's head spun in Jesse's direction. "Stay back!"

Jesse, now less than thirty feet away,

stopped and leaned over the railing. “That’s a long way down.”

The man didn’t answer him; Jesse edged closer. “What’s your name?”

“Harold.”

“Harold what?”

“Harold Bader.”

Jesse was now within ten feet of where the man stood. “Is it alright if I call you Harry?”

“Sure—everyone else does. At least those that still talk to me.”

“Is that why you’re here, Harry. Did people stop talking to you?”

“Yes.”

“Why is that?”

“Because I was listed as 4-F.”

“Your draft status?”

“That’s right.”

Traffic on the bridge was light, but a few cars had stopped, their drivers getting out to help. Jesse did his best to ignore them and focus on Harry. Suddenly, the young man let go, rotated toward the bridge, and grabbed on again.

He was now facing Jesse.

“My father and both my brothers are over there fighting, but I was born hard of hearing. They said I couldn’t serve.”

“But that’s not your fault.”

“I know that, but it’s as if I faked the hearing test or something. Like I wanted to fail and not go.”

Jesse was almost within arm's reach, but instead of trying to grab the man, Jesse climbed over the rail next to him.

Harry stared at Jesse as if he was insane. "What are you doing?"

"Well, if being 4-F is why you're jumping, then I guess I need to go with you."

"What…why?"

"Cause I'm 4-F also."

For the first time, Jesse sensed the man waver in his conviction. Harry seemed to be studying him. "Really?"

"Really. In fact, you wouldn't believe how I ended up 4-F."

A small crowd now surrounded the area, and traffic on the bridge had halted. Harry was curious. "What do you mean?"

"Well, it's like this. You can't fight because of something you were born with, but not me, I can't fight because I got in one."

Harry didn't say anything, just stared, so Jesse continued.

"You see, before the war, I was crazy about this Japanese girl named Keiko. One day, I was visiting the family restaurant, and a high school kid started harassing Keiko's sister. I stepped in and sent the kid packing."

Harry nodded. "Good for you!"

"Yeah, but a few days later, I woke up in the hospital after being beat up by that kid and his friends. One of my injuries was to my eye, the same one that made me 4-F."

Harry let out a whistle. "Wow. You stood up for a Jap, and ended up not being able to fight the Japs. That's nuts!"

Jesse allowed a little smile to cross his face. "That's what I thought!"

"Are people hateful to you as well?"

"Sure, sometimes."

A police car pulled up, and the officer came up behind Harry. Jesse got his attention with a slight shake of his head, which brought the officer to a stop.

Harry didn't notice. "How do you deal with it? The name-calling, the cold shoulders, and stuff like that. Don't you just want to end it all?"

"Sometimes, but I look at it this way. If I were over there fighting to keep my country free, I wouldn't want to come home and learn people had considered my sacrifice something to throw away."

Harry's eyes started to well up and he turned away, staring out toward the bay. When he looked back, his demeanor had changed. "I wouldn't want my dad or brothers to think that."

"Loved ones at home are what this war is all about for those guys on the front line. They'll want you here to greet them when they return."

Harry pulled himself up onto the rail, and the officer came forward quickly to help, placing Harry in handcuffs once he was on solid ground. Jesse climbed back over himself, and the crowd started to cheer.

Jesse ignored the applause and went to the police car. The officer, who had just put Harry in the back, turned to him. "Nice work, young man. What's your name?"

"Jesse."

"Good job, Jesse."

"Thanks. Is Harry under arrest?"

"Technically, but I'll be taking him to Saint Francis for observation."

"How long will he be there?"

"They usually keep them for a couple days."

Jesse bent over so he could see Harry. "Take care of yourself, Harry."

Harry nodded and smiled. "You too."

Jesse watched the police car drive off. It was the best he'd felt in a long, long time.

DECEMBER, 1943

Christmas 1943, was much different than the previous year. Most camp internees now had jobs and some spending money. Many stores had sprung up inside the camp, providing a way for people to decorate their rooms and exchange small gifts.

Roo and Keiko had both been asked to the holiday dance and Keiko, in particular, was excited. She had been seeing Shoji on a regular basis since summer, and dances were one of their favorite things to attend. Roo had a new job in the camp's silkscreen plant, where they printed posters for the Navy, and was going with a boy she'd met there.

The Christmas dance was being held in the dining hall, decorated with streamers of red and green strung across the rafters, and music supplied by the vinyl 78's of Glenn Miller, Bing Crosby, and Keiko's favorite, Count Basie.

At the end of the evening, Shoji walked Keiko back to the barracks. Before they went through the door, he pulled her to the side out of the wind. "I have something for you."

"Ooh…what is it?"

He handed her a small box circled by red string that was tied into a bow. She stared at the tiny package, suddenly afraid of what it might be. When she looked up, he was watching her.

"Open it."

Her fingers trembled as she carefully undid the bow and put the string in her pocket, then lifted the small lid. Inside was a small gold ring, and tears immediately filled her eyes.

Shoji dropped to one knee. "Will you marry me, Keiko?"

She wiped at her eyes, too stunned to answer. Her mind raced to Jesse, and her promise.

She hesitated, frightened she might do the wrong thing. "I don't know what to say…"

Shoji stood. "Say yes."

"I…I can't."

"Why?"

"Not yet, anyway. I need some time."

"Time for what?"

Should she tell him? Would he be angry? Hurt?

"Just to think."

Shoji stood and took the lid, replacing it on the box, then smiled at Keiko. "You keep that, and take as long as you need. When you decide, you put the ring on."

"What if I can't?"

He kissed her cheek. "Then you can return the ring and I'll know your answer."

He walked away, leaving her with the ring, and a heart being torn in two.

MAY, 1944

The winter of 1944 was brutally cold. Finally, the weather had begun to break, and a late spring was at hand. Keiko and Shoji had gone to a dance and were walking back to her barracks, when he stopped her. It was the same as Christmas and she sensed what was coming.

He smiled. "Do you still have the ring?"

"Yes."

"When do you think you will decide?"

She shrugged. "I'm just not sure. If you want me to, I'll give it back."

"No! I told you to take your time and I meant it. I don't want it back unless the answer is no."

Keiko smiled. "Well, I'm not sure—it might be yes."

Shoji laughed. "That's good enough for me."

Shouting from Keiko's barracks interrupted them. Keiko hurried toward the door, walking faster as she got closer. Shoji tried to catch up. "What is it?"

"I don't know. I'll talk to you later."

By now, Keiko had recognized one of the voices doing the shouting—her father.

She rushed down the center hallway, turned into their room, and stopped in her tracks. Sitting on her bed, clutching at her shirt, was Roo. Azumi wiped at her daughter's face with a tea towel.

Pacing frantically back and forth, her father was in a rage. "Who is this boy?"

Roo seemed unable to answer.

Takeshi insisted. "Hotaru! Who was the boy who did this?"

Roo remained silent. Finally grasping what had happened, Keiko blurted out the name.

"Dennis."

Takeshi stopped and stared at his oldest daughter. "Who?"

"Dennis Coleman."

Takeshi looked at Roo. "Is she right?"

Roo managed a nod.

Takeshi turned on Keiko. "You know about this boy?"

"I've spoken to him a couple times about leaving Hotaru alone."

"Well, apparently he ignored you!"

Keiko went to her sister. "Are you okay, Roo?"

Her sister started to cry all over again. "He attacked me!"

"Where?"

"Behind the dining hall."

Takeshi tapped Keiko on the shoulder. "Where can I find this Dennis?"

Keiko looked up at her father.

He wasn't going to like her answer. What if he did something stupid?

There was really no choice. "He's the son of the Camp Administrator."

Her father stared at her, and she could see the implications dawning on him. Jack Coleman was the most powerful man at Heart Mountain. Without another word, he turned and bolted out the door.

****

Roo remained inconsolable for hours, moving from tears to silence, and back again. Keiko tried to take her to the camp hospital but Roo wanted no part of being further humiliated. "I'm not going!"

Keiko did her best to be patient. "Roo, you have to go. We need to make sure you aren't seriously hurt."

Roo was defiant, curled up on her bed. "I'm fine!"

Keiko looked to her mother for help. Azumi went over and sat next to her daughter.

"Hotaru, do you want him to be punished?"

Roo snorted. "He won't get in trouble!"

"Okay, then do you want him to do this to another girl?"

Her daughter rolled over. "No..."

"Then we need to show the authorities what happened by having you checked out."

Roo looked from her mother to her sister. "Will you stay with me?"

Keiko stood. "Every step of the way."

Roo stood and wrapped a blanket around herself. "Okay."

Two hours later, Keiko took her sister to the shower building to get cleaned up. Despite the early morning hour, whispers and stares followed them as they moved around the camp, and it was obvious word of what happened had got out.

When they arrived back at the room, their father and mother were talking in hushed tones on their side of the blanket wall.

Keiko leaned in. "We're back."

Her parents came over to check on Roo. She was laying on her bed when Azumi went to her, caressing her daughter's hand. "How are you feeling?"

Roo didn't answer, instead closing her eyes, and turning toward the wall. Azumi started to cry. Keiko looked at her father, who suddenly looked tired and very old.

"Did you report it?"

He nodded. "Yes."

"What are they going to do?"

Her father walked back to his own cot, dropping onto it with a sigh. "They promised a full investigation."

"Did you tell them what Roo said?"

"Of course."

"And?"

"They said we have to wait until they've got the full story."

"And how long will that be?"

He shrugged. "I don't know."

Her father lay down and rolled toward the wall. His body shook with silent sobs, as Keiko stared at his back. She'd *never* seen her father cry.

****

The wait for an end to the investigation turned out to be short, and when Keiko arrived home from work the next day, she found her mother sitting next to Roo. Her sister was staring at the floor, while her mother held her hand. Father was standing over them, his voice strained.

"I'm sorry, Hotaru, but there's nothing I can do. They're protecting him."

"I understand, Father. I expected as much."

Keiko *didn't* understand. "They aren't going to do anything?"

Her father turned toward her, his eyes sad, contrasting with the anger in his voice. "That's right!"

"Why?"

"They said that it comes down to he said-she said. It's Hotaru's claim of rape against the Coleman boy's claim it was consensual."

"That's crap! Does Roo look like someone who consented?"

Her father's anger flashed, directed at her, but meant for others. "I know it's crap! Don't you think I told them that? What did you want me to do, punch the man?"

"Who?"

"Coleman."

Keiko was incredulous. "The camp administrator handled the investigation of his own son?"

Her father looked away.

Keiko's mind spun as she fought the urge to vomit.

"We've been removed from our homes, shipped around like cattle, caged like animals, and now it's open season on us. Where will it end?"

"I wish I knew, Keiko. I wish I knew."

****

Weeks later, they were all horrified to find out Roo had gotten pregnant from the rape. Since then, Keiko spent most of her time trying to keep her family from dissolving. Eventually, time had passed, and now they focused on making sure the baby was healthy. Azumi even acted excited about becoming a grandmother.

Takeshi wasn't home much, and when he was, Keiko could smell alcohol on him. She'd asked her mother about it.

"Where is Father getting alcohol?"

"What are you talking about?"

She had given her mother a withering look, angry at her for playing dumb. "Come on, Mother. I'm not a child."

Her mother had given her a wry smile, touching Keiko's hair. "No. of course you're not. Some men have found a way to make rice wine with sugar syrup from the fruit cans."

Keiko couldn't fathom how this was done, but it explained alot.

"I wish Father would stay away when he's been drinking."

To Keiko's surprise, her mother agreed. "Me, too."

Keiko found herself spending more and more time with Shoji. Their marriage had begun to feel inevitable, and she carried the ring around with her constantly, but still hadn't put it on.

Often, she would walk out by the fence line and put her hands in her pockets. In one side, she carried the ring. In the other, she would rub her fingers over the seashell from Jesse.

Her life path seemed to be a choice between those two items, but to choose one meant she must throw away the other. For Keiko, it had seemed an impossible decision, until the events surrounding Roo.

Without being aware of it, her perception had shifted to *us* versus *them*. An attitude that would have made her angry back in San Francisco, back when she was with Jesse.

But now, the only justice seemed to come from within her own people, while the pain visited on her came by the hands of her captors.

It was now late June, and on this walk, the flowers moved lazily in the breeze. In between the bright whites and showy pinks of the Bitterroot, stood a single, blue Columbine. Keiko stared down at the lone flower, struck by the symbolism—it was Jesse amongst her people.

Acting on impulse, she bent down and scooped some dirt from around the Columbine. Taking out the shell, she placed it in the tiny hole, and covered it. When she stood up, she removed the ring from the other pocket and slipped it on. She couldn't live torn between two worlds any longer.

JULY, 1944

Jesse sat at the dining table with his mother, drinking coffee and reading the daily paper, which was full of news from France. July fourth was just around the corner, and Jesse had asked a young woman named Rebecca to a picnic sponsored by the church.

As usual, his mother was bringing lots of food, and this morning, she was rolling out some dough. He folded the paper and laid it aside.

"Have you got everything ready for the picnic?"

"Pretty much; just some last-minute baking to do."

"Mom, can I ask you something?"

Estelle stopped and wiped her hands on her checkered apron. "Of course."

"I asked Rebecca to the picnic."

"Oh? Rebecca is a wonderful girl."

"She is, isn't she?"

"You sound unconvinced."

"I don't feel comfortable with it, I guess."

She studied him for several minutes. Finally, she went to the sink and rinsed her hands, then came over and sat opposite him. "You have to let her go, Jesse."

"Keiko?"

"Yes. I know the news was very difficult, and pain like that can make you afraid."

"I keep thinking about that letter. What if it was concocted by her father to separate Keiko and me?"

She took his hand. "Look at me, Jesse."

She waited until he was fully focused on her.

"If you hold on to something like that it will eat you alive. You have to move forward and find your new path."

He stared at her for a long time, then lifted her hand and kissed her fingers. "You're right. Thanks, Mom."

"You're welcome. Good advice is what we mothers are known for."

****

Keiko and Roo sat playing cards in their room on that early July day. The news of an allied invasion had lifted the spirits of the camp, hope rising that the end would be coming soon.

Roo's pregnancy was now prominent, and she liked to tell Keiko when the baby moved. They tried to ignore the events leading up to the pregnancy and focus on the new life coming into the family.

Someone came running down the hallway,

yelling at the top of their lungs.

"Keiko! Keiko!" Shoji burst into the room. "Did you hear?"

"Hear what?"

Shoji stole a glance at Roo, hesitating. "Uh…"

"Out with it, Shoji! What is it?"

"Dennis Coleman is dead."

Keiko wasn't sure she'd heard him correctly. "What did you say?"

"They found Dennis Coleman dead."

"What happened?"

"I'm not sure, but the rumor is he was murdered."

"By who?"

Shoji shrugged.

Keiko looked at Roo, whose lips were curled upward. "Why are you smiling?"

"He got what he deserved!"

"Hotaru, no one *deserves* to be murdered."

Roo put away the cards. "Maybe not, but I'm not going to pretend I'm sad."

Keiko quickly realized suspicion might fall on them.

She stood and pointed at Roo. "You stay here. If Mother or Father come home, make sure they know. Okay?"

"Yes."

"Come on, Shoji. Let's go see what we can find out."

****

Several hours later, Keiko returned to the room to find her mother and Roo sitting close together in hushed conversation. When she entered the room, they looked up with eyes wide in fear. Keiko looked around the room. "Where's Father?"

Her mother shrugged. "I haven't seen him in a while."

"Does he know?"

Another shrug. "I imagine the whole camp knows by now."

Keiko sat on her cot. "Shoji and I have been trying to find out what happened, and if they have a suspect, but no one is talking."

Roo grunted. "It could be any number of people."

It was true. "I imagine Dennis made a lot of enemies."

The door opened and Takeshi slipped in. Azumi went over to where her husband sat perched on an old orange crate. "Where have you been? I was worried sick."

"I had some business to take care of."

"You've heard?"

"Yes."

"Did you learn how it happened or who was responsible?"

"I don't know who did it, but I was told

the boy was strangled."

The word 'strangled' hung in the air, each of them trying to process the ugliness of such an attack. It took a long time to strangle someone, and it was usually personal.

The room remained quiet for the remainder of the evening, and except for a trip to the toilets, no one ventured out.

****

The next several weeks were a blur to Keiko. The U.S. Army Military Police, who had taken over the investigation, questioned both her father and mother. She and Roo were also forced to give statements.

It was the most unnerving thing Keiko had ever gone through.

"Miss Yoshida, please come in."

She'd entered a small office, furnished only with a long table and several chairs, where she was directed to sit at one end. Four men in uniform, their chests glistening with medals, sat around the table. Each had a notepad, and bore matching grave expressions.

In the middle of the table sat a large tape recorder, with microphone cords leading away from it to small standing mics, one in front of each chair. Once she was seated, the man who had escorted her into the room flipped on the recorder. The large reels began to turn.

"Please state your name."

"Keiko Yoshida."

"And your age?"

"Twenty-four."

"And your family number?"

"16573."

"Thank you. Miss Yoshida, my name is Colonel Tompkins, and I am leading the investigation into the death of Dennis Coleman. I'm going to ask you some questions, but you are not under oath, and are free to answer them or not, without suffering any repercussions. However, I encourage you to be truthful. Do you understand?"

"Yes, sir."

"Good, then let's begin. Where were you on the afternoon in question?"

"I was in my barracks with my sister. We were playing cards."

"Your sister is Hotaru Yoshida?"

"Yes."

"Did either of you leave the room at any time that afternoon?"

"No."

"Do you know where your mother, Azumi Yoshida, was at that time?"

"She said she was with some friends at the dining hall."

"She told you that?"

"Yes."

"But you didn't see her there yourself?"

Keiko was surprised by the question. The idea her mother could be capable of murder was preposterous to Keiko, and she hadn't thought twice about where her mother had been.

"My mother could never hurt anyone."

"Please answer the question."

"No, I didn't personally see her at the hall."

"Thank you. Your father's name is Takeshi Yoshida, correct?"

"Yes."

"Do you know of his whereabouts on the afternoon in question?"

"Not really."

The men around the table exchanged glances. A sense of dread filled her as the Colonel leaned forward. "Not really? Would you clarify that for us, please?"

"Well, he said he had some business to take care of."

The moment the words left her mouth, she realized the impact of what she'd said. The men all began to write on their pads, whispering to each other, and then writing some more.

Keiko wanted to burst into tears.

After what seemed like an eternity, the questions continued. "When was the first time you saw your father that afternoon?"

"Around dinnertime."

"Did you notice anything different about

him?"

"What do you mean by different?"

"Was he nervous, upset, angry?"

Keiko fought to keep her composure. "No."

"Nothing?"

"No!"

The colonel looked at the other men, then turned the recorder off.

"Thank you for your time, Miss Yoshida. You may go."

Keiko bolted from the room, afraid she'd done terrible harm to her father.

Afterward, her father had asked her about the questioning.

"Are you okay, Daughter?"

"Yes."

But that was it. He didn't push for details or make her recount the interview.

In the days following her own questioning, Keiko learned dozens of people in the camp were being interviewed, and she began to hope the paranoia about her own testimony might be overblown.

Perhaps this will all go away soon.

Her optimism would soon be shattered.

AUGUST, 1944

On a hot August morning before dawn, heavy boots thumped down the barracks hallway, followed by the door of their room bursting open. Keiko bolted upright, her heart in her throat.

A soldier took up a position next to the bed, pointing a rifle at her.

"Stay down! Stay in your bed!"

Roo screamed as another soldier pointed his gun at her, telling her to shut up.

A muffled cry from their mother came through the blanket wall, followed by the shouting of a third soldier. "Don't move, lady!"

A scuffle followed, then her father's voice. "What is the meaning of this?"

"Takeshi Yoshida, you're under arrest for the murder of Dennis Coleman."

"What? That's crazy! You've got the wrong man!"

Moments later, her father came bursting through the blanket wall, his hands cuffed behind him, a fourth soldier pushing him toward the door. The other three soldiers backed out after them, then the door slammed closed. They had come and gone in less than a minute.

"Keiko! Hotaru! Are you okay?"

The girls jumped from their beds and ran to their mother. She was curled up in the corner, tears streaming down her face, and they huddled together on the floor. The three of them remained there for nearly an hour, paralyzed by fear.

Eventually, Keiko ventured out to get some food, then returned, reporting to her mother the looks and whispers she'd endured.

"No one seems to know what to say or do. They look at me, then divert their eyes when I nod."

A knock came at the door and all three jumped. Keiko moved over by the door and leaned against the frame. "Who is it?"

"My name is Michio Toma. I'm a lawyer."

"What do you want with us?"

"I've been assigned to defend your father."

Keiko swung the door wide. "I'm sorry, Mr. Toma. We're a little on edge today."

"Perfectly understandable."

The young man, Keiko guessed twenty-eight or twenty-nine, was polite, clean-cut, and reserved. He shuffled through the door, and waited for it to be closed before speaking again.

"Is Mrs. Yoshida here?"

"Yes," Keiko pointed beyond the curtain. "This way."

Keiko introduced the lawyer to Roo and her mother, then offered Mr. Toma a seat. He set his briefcase down and unbuttoned his suit coat, but remained standing. He addressed himself to their mother.

"Mrs. Yoshida, I have been appointed to defend your husband against the charge of second-degree murder in the death of Dennis Coleman."

"Thank you, Mr. Toma. Do you know what evidence they base this charge on? We haven't been told anything."

"So far, all I've learned is they have two witnesses, both of whom say they saw your father arguing with the victim on the day in question."

"Witnesses? Who are these witnesses?"

"I don't have their names, but I will eventually be able to question them. In addition to the witnesses, your husband has apparently not provided an alibi for the time of the murder. Can you help me with that?"

Their mother shrugged. "Not really. I can't say for certain where my husband was."

The lawyer turned toward the girls. "What about you two? Can you vouch for your father's whereabouts?"

Keiko and Roo both shrugged. Mr. Toma zeroed in on Roo.

"Is it true you reported a sexual attack by the deceased?"

"Yes."

"And what was the result of that report?"

"Father said they couldn't do anything because it was my word against the boy's."

The lawyer glanced at Roo's oversized stomach, then nodded. He turned back to Azumi.

"They're claiming vengeance was your husband's motive for the murder."

Keiko wasn't surprised. "Mr. Toma, there's a long list of people who didn't like Dennis Coleman. He wasn't a nice person."

"I've got that impression from others, and it'll be part of our defense, but right now I need information. I'm going to ask each of you a series of questions, and I want you to answer them as completely and honestly as possible. Don't leave anything out, no matter how small you think it is. Then, after I leave, you need to go over the questions again to make sure you haven't forgotten anything."

The women all nodded, so Mr. Toma opened his briefcase and pulled out a notepad. "Let's start with you, Mrs. Yoshida."

****

As Christmas approached, Keiko's father was still being held without bail, away from the camp in the county jail. Her mother had been allowed to visit, but not his daughters, and now word had come the trial wouldn't be held until after the first of the year.

Mr. Toma had kept them up to date on developments and carried messages to their father, but the lawyer had made one thing clear—he wasn't optimistic about the trial's outcome. He said the witnesses and circumstantial evidence were compelling. Keiko wasn't sure what to believe anymore.

Shoji had asked if she would be ready to marry before Christmas, and took the news she wanted to wait until after the trial with his usual calm, despite his obvious disappointment. Otherwise, he'd been steady as a rock by her side, lifting her up when she was down, and even spending time with Roo.

One afternoon in early December, Keiko arrived from work to find her mother sitting alone in their room, sobbing. "Mother? Are you okay?"

Her mother turned around and patted the spot next to her on the cot. "Come here, Daughter. I have something to tell you."

Keiko's mouth went dry and her pulse pounded as she sat down. Her mother was turning a piece of paper over and over in her hands. "What is that, Mother?"

"It's something I've saved for a long while, and the time has come to give it to you, but first you have to understand something."

"Of course, Mother. What is it?"

Azumi now looked directly into her

daughter's eyes, tears still running down her face. "I want you to know that everything your father did, every decision he made, was because he thought it was in your best interest."

A chill worked its way up Keiko's spine, like a crawling dread she wanted to crush before it got to her brain. "What decision, Mother?"

Azumi looked one more time at the card, handed it to Keiko, then turned away. Keiko held the card in her hand, trying to make sense out of what it said.

SANTA ANITA ASSEMBLY CENTER

VISITATION CONFIRMATION

FAMILY NAME - YOSHIDA

FAMILY NUMBER - 16573

VISITOR NAME - JESSE SOMMERS

APPROVED DATE - JUNE 4, 1942

APPROVED TIME - 3:00

"Is this real?"

Her mother didn't turn around. "Yes."

"Did Jesse come to the appointment?"

Her mother nodded, wiping her eyes.

"What happened? Why wasn't I told?"

"Your father met with Jesse. He told him you were sick, then asked him not to contact you anymore."

Keiko's blood ran cold.

It's not possible! Jesse had come to see her after all? How could father do this to her?

"Why didn't you tell me sooner?"

"I promised your father I wouldn't."

A fire seared her consciousness, sparked by anger, and stoked by pain. "So you let me say yes to Shoji, knowing Jesse still cared?"

"It's been over two years. I figured Jesse had moved on by now, at least, that's what your father believed."

Keiko refused to restrain the anger inside. "What else is there to tell me? Is there more?"

"Your father made me…" Azumi faltered. "Oh, Keiko…it's too awful."

"Mother!" Keiko didn't care if everyone in the camp heard. "Tell me!"

"Your father returned the letters intended for you…"

"And?"

"And Jesse was told you were dead."

Keiko rocked back visibly, as if hit by a punch. She couldn't catch her breath. The room spun, and she grabbed the side of the cot to keep from falling over.

Roo came through the door and froze at the sight in front of her. "What's going on?"

Keiko stood and looked down at her mother. "How could you?"

She brushed past Roo, headed for the door. Roo staggered sideways. "Will someone tell me what is going on?"

Keiko stopped and pointed at her mother. "Ask her. I don't have the stomach to repeat it."

She grabbed her notepaper and raced from the room, headed for the outer fence.

One thought coursed through her.

She must write Jesse. She had to know if he still loved her!

DECEMBER, 1944

Christmas was just a couple days away as Jesse went over a file at his desk. Uncle Jerry was at lunch, and Jesse planned to leave after his uncle returned, taking the rest of the day off. The phone rang, and after a brief conversation, Janet swiveled in her chair. "It's for you. It's your mother."

"Thanks.

Jesse picked up the phone and leaned back in his chair. "Hi, Mom."

"Hi, Son. Are you busy?"

The strain in her voice compelled him sit forward. "Not really. Is something wrong?"

"Can you get away?"

"Sure, why?"

"I have…there's something you need to see."

"What is it?"

"It's a…just come home as soon as you can."

The line went dead and Jesse was left staring at the receiver. Janet noticed the look on his face. "Is everything okay?"

Jesse hung up the phone, closed the file on his desk, and headed for the door.

"Tell my uncle I had to leave and I'll call him later."

He didn't wait for a response before bolting for his car.

****

Twenty minutes later, Jesse arrived home. When he entered the house, his mother was pacing in the kitchen, her words running together, not making sense. "There…you'll see...there…it's right there…I can't believe it."

"What are you talking about? What's right there?"

At first, he didn't spot the envelope, but his eye was drawn to its familiar handwriting. His knees started to give out. Grabbing a chair and catching himself before he made it to the floor, he sat in front of the letter, and slid it toward him.

He'd know her handwriting anywhere, but how could it be?

He checked the postmark.

December nineteenth—just four days ago!

He sat staring at the date, not moving, until his mother sat across from him. "Aren't you going to open it?"

He looked up, his eyes glazed over. "Sure...but how?"

His mother shrugged, regarding the letter

like a snake ready to strike.

Slowly, delicately, almost as if it might evaporate, Jesse peeled open the flap. Inside was an entire page written in the beautiful script of Keiko's hand. Jesse's eyes went immediately to the bottom.

All my love, Keiko.

His eyes filled with tears, and his hands began trembling.

She still loved him!

Going back to the beginning, he read silently as his mother watched him.

My Dearest Jesse,

As I write this letter, I can't begin to fathom what it will be like for you to receive it. Obviously, I did not die as you were told. My father is responsible for that horrific lie, and I hate him for it, but he has his own troubles now.

I found out everything, including about your visit to Santa Anita, from my mother today. I didn't know what else to do but write. I wanted you to know the truth. I'm alive, and more importantly, I have never stopped loving you.

You may have moved on, in fact, you probably have. I have made new friends too, and even got engaged to a nice boy. We've not set the date, and if I'm honest with myself, you're the reason why I keep procrastinating. I've never forgotten you.

I'll wait to hear from you, and if I don't, I will understand.

All my love, Keiko.

Jesse let the letter slide out of his hands and onto the table. Tears rolled down his face, and unable to read it aloud, he pushed it toward his mother. She read it, then looked up at him with red eyes. "You were right."

Jesse nodded, then buried his face in his hands.

****

The next day, Jesse sat at the kitchen table and called his uncle. "Hey, Jerry."

"Morning, Jesse. Are you running late?"

"No. I need the day off."

"What's up?"

"I received a letter from Keiko yesterday."

There was a long pause on the other end of the phone.

"Wow. She's okay?"

"Yes."

His uncle was understanding as always. "Don't worry about coming in. You get things straightened out. It's Christmas Eve, so I'll probably close early anyway."

"Thanks, Jerry."

Jesse's uncle was aware of his nephew's feelings for Rebecca. "What are you going to tell Rebecca?"

Jesse and Rebecca had been dating for nearly six months and marriage had already come up. "I don't know, Uncle. I just don't know."

"Will we still see you and Estelle for Christmas dinner?"

"Yes. I'll talk to you later."

Jesse hung up and took the cup of coffee his mother offered him. "Thanks."

They'd spent most of the previous evening sitting in this same spot, the letter lying on the table between them. Occasionally, one of them would pick it up, read it again, and shake their head.

Jesse looked up at his mother, who didn't appear to have slept any more than he had. "What should I do?"

"I can't tell you that, Jesse. I know you've been praying about it all night, and there's a lot at stake, but you have to follow your heart. What is it telling you?"

Jesse gave her a wry smile. "My heart is no help! It still loves Keiko but doesn't want to lose Rebecca."

"My guess is your heart loves Keiko, but your *mind* is afraid to lose Rebecca."

"You may be right, but what do I do about it?"

"Like I said, that's for you to decide. I'm not going to be the one who has to live with the decision, so I'm not the one who should make it."

Jesse laughed. "You should have been a politician! You'd make Harry Truman proud!"

****

Keiko strolled with Roo out by the perimeter fence. Roo had started to join Keiko's walks, and they often spent the time encouraging each other, when the weather wasn't too cold. Roo would walk for a while and then need to sit, as her swollen ankles were beginning to bother her. Keiko would drop down beside her. "How are you feeling?"

"Tired, fat."

"You're very brave."

Roo stared at her sister. "I don't have much choice!"

Keiko laughed. "I suppose that's true."

"Have you and Mother spoken yet?"

Keiko shook her head. "No."

"You can't stay angry at her, Keiko. You know Father is the one who's responsible."

"I know. It might be easier if Father was here, so I could focus my anger on him, but looking at Mother just reminds me of what they did."

Roo shifted uncomfortably. "Are you going to attend Father's trial?"

"I guess I have to, especially since we almost certainly will have to testify."

"Do you think he did it?"

Roo hadn't posed the question before now, and although Keiko had spent a lot of time wondering that very thing, she still wasn't sure of the answer.

"I don't know. Part of me thinks Father is capable of it, and part of me doesn't."

They sat quietly for a long time before Roo turned to her. "Have you heard anything from Jesse?"

Keiko shook her head slowly. "I'm afraid it's over."

"I'm sorry."

Keiko stood and helped her sister to her feet. "Me, too."

****

Keiko was stretched out on her cot one day in early January when a knock came at the door. "Yes?"

"It's me!"

Keiko got up and let Shoji in, then returned to her cot. He was not his normal, happy self.

"What's wrong, Shoji?"

He dropped down on the cot and handed her a piece of paper. Keiko had seen ones like it many times—a draft notice. "When do you have to report?"

"Next week."

"I'm sorry, Shoji."

"It's okay. I want to fight for my country, but I want us to marry before I leave."

Keiko was a step ahead of him, and had already considered the possibility.

"I don't know."

"Keiko, we've been engaged for months. It's time, please, before I go."

The decision was clear, but that made it no easier. Shoji was a good man who deserved better than a woman who didn't love him. Slipping the ring off her finger, she placed it in his palm, and curled his fingers around it. "I'm sorry, Shoji. I can't"

The young man stared at her through reddening eyes. "I expected as much. Goodbye, Keiko."

He kissed her cheek and left. Despite knowing it was the right path, Keiko lay down and cried, as much for Shoji as herself.

JANUARY, 1945

The trial of Takeshi Yoshida finally began on January Sixteenth and opened to a packed courtroom. Held in the dining hall, people had lined up early to get a seat, despite the brutal cold. Keiko, her mother, and a very pregnant Hotaru were in the front row, directly behind Takeshi.

Her father had arrived by car from the county jail and been led into the courtroom with his hands cuffed in front of him. He eye's searched each member of the family, but Keiko avoided his look. Roo sat between Keiko and their mother, whose hand occasionally lifted a handkerchief to her face, dabbing at the corners of her eyes.

Judge Christopher Weldon was announced to the room and everyone stood. He was a short man with gray, receding hair, and bright, serious eyes. He sat down, followed by the rest of the room, and went straight to work. "Takeshi Yoshida, please stand."

Her father stood, teetering slightly, like his knees might give out. "Yes, your Honor?"

"You're charged with the second-degree murder of Dennis Coleman. How do you plead?"

"Not guilty, your Honor."

"And I understand you have requested a bench trial, is that correct?"

"Yes, your Honor."

"You understand that I will be the sole person to decide your guilt or innocence?"

"I do, your Honor."

"Very well, you may be seated."

Her father dropped back into his chair. Judge Weldon gestured toward the bailiff. "Remove those cuffs, please."

Takeshi rubbed his wrists when the restraints were removed.

Roo leaned over to Keiko. "Why did he choose a bench trial?"

"The jury would have come from the citizens outside the camp. Mister Toma didn't think he could get an impartial jury."

There was a commotion in the back of the courtroom as the parents of Dennis Coleman made their entrance. They shook hands, walking down the center of the aisle as if they were arriving royalty, as the judge banged his gavel repeatedly. When they were finally seated, Judge Weldon glared at the prosecutor. "Who are these people?"

Prosecutor Benjamin Gibbins looked dismayed. "The victim's family, your Honor."

The judge addressed the Mr. and Mrs. Coleman directly.

"I will not tolerate interruptions in my

courtroom like the spectacle I just witnessed. In the future, you will be seated before the proceedings begin, is that clear?"

Mr. Coleman nodded. "Yes, your Honor."

Judge Weldon turned his attention back to the prosecutor. "Mr. Gibbins, you can call your first witness."

"Thank you, your Honor. The State calls George Miller, the county coroner."

Keiko watched the man enter the courtroom and move to the front, the first in a long series of prosecution experts. The morning dragged on with a string of medical people, police officers, military officials, and finally, Colonel Tompkins.

Tompkins, who'd led the murder investigation, was the one whose testimony revealed the accusation of rape by Hotaru against Dennis Coleman. There was an audible gasp in the room, and all eyes turned to her sister. Roo's eyes remained fixed directly ahead, focusing on the back of her father.

Court finally broke for lunch, and Keiko had still not seen the witnesses she wanted to hear most—the people who identified her father as arguing with Dennis on the day he was murdered. She didn't have to wait long after the break.

"The State calls Etsuko Fujita."

A woman, who could have been the twin of Keiko's own mother, walked slowly from the back of the room. A deathly silence fell over the room, only broken by the swirling wind against the windows. As she reached the witness chair, she raised her hand and swore '*to tell the truth, the whole truth, and nothing but the truth.*'

Prosecutor Gibbins got out of his seat. "Please state your name."

"Etsuko Fujita."

"And your family number?"

"19368."

"Thank you. Now Mrs. Fujita, can you tell us where you were around the time that Dennis Coleman was killed?"

"I was returning from the laundry building."

"Were you alone?"

"No. My daughter was with me."

"Can you tell me what you witnessed?"

Keiko didn't take her eyes off the woman, but Etsuko never looked at her or her father.

The woman's voice quivered as she continued. "I saw two men arguing."

"And where was this argument taking place?"

"Between barracks 26 and 27."

"Did you know either of the men?"

"Yes. One was Dennis Coleman."

"And do you see the other in this courtroom today?"

The woman's eyes remained focused on the prosecutor as she pointed in the direction of

Keiko's father. "Yes. That's him."

The prosecutor returned to his desk. "Let the court note that she pointed at the defendant, Takeshi Yoshida. Was this a heated argument?"

"Heated?"

"Yes. Angry, physical."

"Yes, I would say so."

"Thank you. No further questions."

Michio Toma stood, came around his desk, and approached Mrs. Fujita. She appeared afraid of him, leaning slightly away, while still focusing on the prosecutor. Toma stopped directly in front of her, forcing the woman to look at him.

"Mrs. Fujita, I noticed that when you identified my client as the man you saw, you didn't look at him. Are you sure it was Mr. Yoshida?"

"Yes, I'm sure."

Toma moved over in front of Judge Weldon. "Your Honor, I would ask that the court instruct the witness to look at the defendant when she identifies him, to be sure we have the correct man."

The prosecutor jumped to his feet. "Your Honor, I object. This is unnecessary theatrics!"

The judge looked at Takeshi, then Mrs. Fujita. "Objection overruled. Mr. Toma, you may ask for a new identification."

"Thank you, your Honor. Mrs. Fujita, is the man you saw arguing with Dennis Coleman, on the day in question, here in the room?"

"Yes."

"Would you look at him now and point at him."

The woman seemed to shrink, nearly disappearing behind the judge's bench, and broke into tears when she looked at Keiko's father. Her arm seemed to hang in the air for a moment, before coming to rest, pointing at Takeshi. "Him."

Tears poured down her face as she quickly looked away. Toma waited for her to compose herself before asking his next question.

"Mrs. Fujita, you said you recognized the other man as Dennis Coleman, correct?"

"Yes."

"How was it that you were familiar with Mr. Coleman?"

"I had seen him talking to my daughter."

Toma stopped and considered her answer. It was obvious to Keiko that he hadn't expected the response. Toma moved over by the defense table and leaned on it.

"Can you tell me, Mrs. Fujita, did your daughter have a relationship with Dennis Coleman?"

The woman's eyes flashed angrily, and she spit her words toward Toma. "Absolutely not!"

Mr. Toma let the words hang in the courtroom, sensing their impact, and letting them linger. He had managed to show the court how people felt about Dennis without directly asking anyone.

"Mrs. Fujita, you said the argument you witnessed between my client and Mr. Coleman was heated, is that right?"

"Yes, angry."

"Did you see Mr. Yoshida attack Dennis Coleman?"

"No."

"Did you see Mr. Yoshida push or strike Mr. Coleman?"

"No."

Toma paused.

"Tell me, Mrs. Fujita, was Dennis Coleman alive the last time you saw him?"

"I'm sorry?"

"Was...Dennis...Coleman...alive the last time you saw him?"

"Yes."

"So you didn't witness a murder, you witnessed an argument, is that correct?"

"Yes."

"Do you regularly see arguments between people here in the camp?"

"Yes, I suppose so."

"Why did this argument stand out in your mind?"

"I don't know. It just did."

"I see," The attorney turned toward the judge. "Your Honor, the defense will concede my client is guilty of being in an argument, but that is a far cry from murder. No further questions."

The judge excused the woman, and the tension as she walked out of the courtroom was thick in the air. Keiko couldn't take anymore, and despite the next witness being the Fujita's daughter, she got up and went for a walk. She had no doubt the woman was lying.

An hour later, Roo found her in the barracks. "The prosecution rested. The judge said Mr. Toma could call his first witness in the morning."

"How did it go with the daughter?"

"Almost exactly the same as Mrs. Fujita. It was as if they were reading from the same script."

"So, I guess it's our time to testify tomorrow. Are you ready?"

Roo shrugged. "I'll tell you what I'm very ready for—I'm ready for this baby to be born!"

Keiko laughed, enjoying the brief moment of distraction. "I don't doubt it. You look like you're hiding a football in there!"

Roo swiped at her, missing. "Thanks! You really know how to hurt a girl. You'll have your turn, you just wait."

"I hope so. Someday."

****

The next morning, the scene from the previous day repeated itself. The only difference was the presence of the Mr. and Mrs. Coleman *before* the judge arrived. Judge Weldon got right down to business. “Mr. Toma, you may call your first witness.”

“Your Honor, the defense calls Azumi Yoshida.”

Keiko watched her mother walk to the stand, and was surprised not to detect any fear. When she was sworn in, her voice was clear and calm. Toma gave her smile, then began the questioning with the basics. Eventually, he got to his key point.

“Mrs. Yoshida, do you know where your husband was at the time of the murder?”

“He was with a friend making rice wine.”

The courtroom started to buzz, and even Keiko was surprised. The attorney turned to look at the people in the court, waiting for quiet, before asking his next question. The judge pounded his gavel until order was restored.

Michio continued. “Mrs. Yoshida, isn’t making rice wine illegal at Heart Mountain?”

“Yes.”

“And is this why your husband did not reveal what he was doing to the police?”

“I believe so, yes.”

“Do you know who the friend was?”

“I do not.”

“Mrs. Yoshida, has your husband ever

physically harmed you or your daughters?"

"Never."

"Would you describe your husband as a violent man?"

"Absolutely not."

"Thank you. No further questions."

The prosecutor stood. "Mrs. Yoshida, did you see your husband involved in this wine making that day?"

"No."

"And so the knowledge he was doing this, at the time of the murder, came from where?"

"Takeshi told me."

"Your husband told you."

"Yes."

"No further questions, your Honor."

Her mother returned to her seat as Michio Toma called his next witness.

"The defense calls Keiko Yoshida."

Her heart pounding, she made her way to the witness chair, and was sworn in.

"Please state your name."

"Keiko Yoshida."

The judge interrupted. "You'll have to speak up."

Her response was almost a yell. "Yes, sir. Keiko Yoshida!"

Michio smiled, then had her give the family number and her age.

"Miss Yoshida, how would you describe your father?"

Keiko looked at Takeshi, whose eyes were fixed on her, and was taken aback by how small he seemed. Her father had always been a giant in her eyes, the authority and stability in her world, a force in her life she'd taken for granted. But now, he looked tiny and afraid, hardly like a murderer.

"He has always been there for my mother, myself, and my sister. He had our best interest in his heart at all times."

Her father started to weep, and the realization that came with her own words washed over her. She forced herself not to cry.

"Would you describe your father as a violent man?"

"No."

"Has he ever struck you?"

"No!"

"Have you ever seen him strike your mother or your sister?"

"Definitely not."

"Thank you. No further questions."

Prosecutor Gibbins stood, but remained at his table.

"Miss Yoshida, I would like to read something to you. It's part of the transcript from your interview with Colonel Tompkins."

He picked up a sheet of paper, and as Keiko held her breath, he began.

"Colonel Tompkins: Do you know of your father's whereabouts on the afternoon in question?

Your response: Not really.

Colonel Tompkins: Not really? Would you clarify that for us, please?

Your response: Well, he said he had some business to take care of."

Again, the courtroom began to hum with whispers. Again, the judge brought order with his gavel.

The prosecutor continued. "Are those your words, Miss Yoshida?"

"Yes, as I recall."

"He said 'he had some business to take care of'. Is that accurate?"

Keiko looked at her father, her heart breaking, her own words haunting her. "Yes."

"Do you know what this 'business' was?"

"No."

"No further questions, your Honor."

Keiko was excused and returned to her seat.

Most people expected her father to take the stand in his own defense, but that would not be the case.

When Michio asked Takeshi if he wanted to testify, her father had shook his head.

"I have nothing to defend myself against. I did no wrong."

Toma had changed his mind about calling Hotaru because of the inflammatory nature of her pregnancy. He'd explained it to the family several days ago.

"Even though it may add justification to your father's actions, if people believed she was raped, in the eyes of the judge it might only reaffirm his guilt. With a jury it might make a difference, but the judge is only concerned with 'if' your father killed Coleman, not 'why' he did."

Michio Toma stood at the defense table, and with no other choice, rested their case.

Judge Weldon stood. "I will hear final arguments tomorrow morning at nine."

His gavel dropped and court was over.

****

At nine sharp, the prosecutor delivered his final statement. He laid out the case step by step, insisting there was no one else with motive, opportunity, and means.

He hammered away specifically at the prosecution's theory of motive—the rape.

When it was his turn, Michio Toma walked to the center of the courtroom.

"Your Honor, despite the circumstantial evidence that indicates my client *may* have committed this crime, it does not rise to the level of proving he *did* commit the crime. Specifically, the State has failed to prove it beyond a reasonable doubt."

Michio walked over and stood by Takeshi, the courtroom silent except for his footsteps.

"What we do know, beyond a shadow of a doubt, is that Dennis Coleman was alive the last time he was seen with Mr. Yoshida. We also know there was no evidence of a struggle on any of my client's clothing or on his person. And finally, we know Takeshi Yoshida is not a violent man."

The lawyer went over by the prosecution table and stopped, looking at the Coleman family.

"What happened to these poor people's son is horrific, but in the effort to seek justice, we must make sure we don't create a greater injustice. The suggested motive is enough to make any person's blood boil, but that is not proof of a crime."

Michio Toma moved to directly in front of Judge Weldon.

"And therefore, your Honor, I ask you to find Takeshi Yoshida innocent."

Toma walked quickly to the defense table and sat down.

Judge Weldon looked over the courtroom as the silence pressed down on everyone. He let his gaze move around the chamber without actually making eye contact with anyone.

Finally, he stood. "I will take this case into consideration, and issue my decision in the next week to ten days. Thank you all for your cooperation. Court is dismissed."

Michio turned around to Keiko. "Well, now we wait."

"What do you think?"

He shrugged. "Best guess? 50-50."

FEBRUARY, 1945

Two weeks passed before word came the judge had decided the case. The dining hall was full nearly two hours before the scheduled time of ten in the morning, with many more curious bystanders milling around outside.

Keiko could feel the eyes staring at them as she, Roo, and their mother moved down the center aisle toward their seats. The Colemans were already seated, refusing to look at the Yoshidas. Mr. Toma had smiled at them when they came in, but hadn't spoken, and Keiko could sense his nervousness.

Her father, on the other hand, appeared calm as he sat quietly at the defense table. He had been brought in just before ten, his handcuffs removed, and then seated next to his lawyer.

Keiko hadn't slept at all the previous night. Over and over, she played out the two possible outcomes, trying to prepare herself for this morning. Now, she sat frozen and afraid.

Like Father, her mother appeared calm, but Keiko sensed it was born out of resignation. Since the trial ended, her mother had repeated the same thing to everyone who asked what she thought the decision would be. "*Shikata ga nai.*"

At precisely ten, the bailiff walked into the court and announced the judge, whose face bore no sign of the decision to come. Once everyone was seated, he looked out over the courtroom. After what seemed an eternity to Keiko, he finally turned his gaze to her father.

"Takeshi Yoshida, please stand."

Her father rose, the scraping of his chair the only sound in the room. Michio Toma stood as well. The three Yoshida women joined hands, bracing themselves.

"It is the decision of this court that you, Takeshi Yoshida, are guilty…"

The rest of Judge Weldon's words were drowned out by the uproar. Keiko sat numb and disbelieving, her eyes fixed on the back of her father. Roo immediately started to cry, and her mother put her face in her hands. Despite the commotion around him, Takeshi hadn't moved, his eyes remaining on the judge.

For his part, Judge Weldon was banging his gavel so hard that Keiko was amazed it didn't break. It took a full ten minutes to restore order within the building, and all the while, her father stood motionless.

Eventually, the room fell quiet again, and Judge Weldon returned his focus to her father.

"Mr. Yoshida, do you have anything you'd like to say before I sentence you?"

"Yes, your Honor."

Slowly, Takeshi turned until he was looking directly at his family. "I want my wife and daughters to know I did not do this terrible thing. Be strong, and trust the truth will find its way out."

The room seemed to be holding its collective breath. Next, he looked at the Coleman family.

"Mr. and Mrs. Coleman, I extend my sympathies for your loss and can't imagine your pain. I want to assure you *I* am not the one who hurt your son."

Keiko looked at the Colemans, who were staring straight ahead, refusing to acknowledge her father. Their faces remained grim, and they said nothing.

Finally, her father turned back to Judge Weldon.

"I know your Honor has done as he sees best, and I wish you no ill, but I stand before you with a clear conscience."

Her father lifted his chin, clasped his hands behind his back, and waited.

Judge Weldon nodded. "Very well. The court imposes a sentence of thirty years, to be served in the Wyoming State Penitentiary at Rawlins. Bailiff, remand the defendant to custody."

The gavel fell for the last time, and the judge was gone. And so was her father.

****

Two days later, Roo gave birth to a baby boy. She named him Jomei Takeshi. Keiko was smitten with her nephew. "Where did you get the name, Roo?"

"Jomei means to spread light. We've experienced such darkness in the last few months, and I believe this baby is here to push that darkness away."

"I think it's great."

A few days later, the little child was home in the barracks, and had become JT. Azumi threw herself into being a grandmother, allowing the distraction to push away the pain of the trial. They all began to look beyond the camp to life outside the wire fences.

Keiko had two things filling her mind in the days after the trial. The first was checking for a letter from Jesse, which appeared less and less likely with every passing day. The second was preparing the family to leave Heart Mountain. They had been given train tickets to return to San Francisco, along with twenty-five dollars each, and were set to travel as soon as JT and Roo were able.

Around two thousand of their fellow internees had already left, and the reports from the coast said things were good for them, despite a few incidents of resentment. Many others still in camp didn't have a clear idea of what to do, or where they would go.

Some had taken farm jobs outside the camp and were staying in Wyoming, an idea her mother had approached Keiko about.

"Do you want to stay on here in Wyoming? There's a poultry factory hiring near here."

"Not a chance!"

Her mother had laughed. "Okay, but why?"

"I am not putting up with one more winter in this forsaken countryside. I want to go back to where it's warm!"

From the next room, Roo had chimed in. "I'm on board with that plan. These winters are horrible!"

Her mother's smile had disappeared. "It means being far from your father."

Keiko took her mother's hand. "I know, but San Francisco is our home. When he gets out, he'll return there, too."

"You're right. And with blessings, father will get out soon. Mr. Toma is planning to appeal."

"Then it's settled. The doctor said Roo would be released to travel next week."

Her mother's voice had dropped to a whisper. "Will you go with me to tell your father?"

"Of course."

****

The morning to leave turned out to be Valentine's Day. On the day before, Michio Toma picked up Keiko and her mother for the ride into town. Takeshi had not yet been moved to the State Penitentiary, and the ride to the county jail was short.

Although allowed into the detention area, where they stood in front of Takeshi's cell, they were forbidden to make physical contact. Keiko was taken aback at her father's appearance. He was gaunt and pale. "Are you okay, Father?"

He forced a smile. "I will be fine, Daughter. I am so glad to see you."

Azumi was quietly crying next to Keiko. She managed a tearful "I love you," but that was about all she could get out.

"Is Hotaru with you?"

Keiko shook her head. "She is back at the camp with JT."

The mention of his grandson seemed to rock her father backwards, but he recovered quickly. "I hear the camp is closing."

"Yes. We came to tell you of our plans."

"And?"

"We have decided to return home to San Francisco."

Her father stared at her for a long time

before nodding his head. "That is a wise decision, Daughter. If I get released from prison, I will join you there."

"*When* Father, *when* you get released."

For the first time in longer than Keiko could remember, her father laughed.

"Yes, Daughter. When."

****

Jesse sat in his bedroom, re-reading the letter from Keiko for the thousandth time. Rebecca was coming over for dinner, and he had to decide what to do. A knock at the door interrupted his thoughts, so he laid the letter on his dresser, and went to answer it.

When he opened the door, Rebecca was standing there in the red dress she'd worn the first Christmas they were together. "You look wonderful."

"Thank you, sir." She tugged at his jacket's lapel. "Nice suit."

He smiled. "Thanks. Mom has dinner ready."

Dinner with Estelle had become a regular event, especially around holidays, and Valentine's was no different. Rebecca had been supportive ever since Jesse took her aside.

"Holidays are the hardest for Mom."

"You mean without your father?"

"Yeah, even Valentine's Day and July Fourth. I think it's because father made such a big deal out of them."

"It's no problem, Jesse. We can have our private moments other times."

"Thanks."

And so it had been for the last few years. Dinner that night included his mother's Banana Nut bread, one of Rebecca's favorites. Jesse had taken a piece and gone to the living room with his coffee. Rebecca called out from the kitchen. "Jesse?"

"Yeah?"

"I need a pencil to write down your mother's recipe."

"On my dresser!"

A few minutes later, Rebecca rushed through the living room. She had her coat on and went straight to the door. Jesse looked up in surprise. "Where are you going?"

"To get some air."

The door slammed.

Jesse got up and went into the kitchen. His mother was sitting at the table, the letter from Keiko lying in front of her. Jesse recognized instantly what had happened.

Turning, he ran for the door, getting outside just as Rebecca started her car. "Rebecca!"

She started to back out as Jesse banged on her window. "Rebecca!"

She stopped and rolled down the window slightly. "What?"

"Can't we talk about it?"

"What's there to talk about?"

Jesse hadn't grabbed a coat and was shivering. "Will you please come back inside?"

"No."

"Then can I get in the car?"

Reluctantly, she leaned across and unlocked the passenger door. Jesse scrambled around and climbed in. He rubbed his arms, trying to warm up. "I meant to tell you about the letter."

"But you didn't."

"No."

"Did you write her back?"

"No."

"We're you *planning* to write her back?"

"I don't know."

"Do you still love her?"

Jesse was under no illusions.

If he said yes, he'd lose Rebecca forever. If he said no…he'd be lying to her and himself.

"Yes."

"Goodbye, Jesse."

There was no point in arguing with her. In fact, just admitting out loud his true feelings lifted a burden off him.

He pulled the door handle and climbed out. "I'm sorry, Rebecca."

She looked at him with tears in her eyes.

"I am too, Jesse."
He closed the door and she was gone.

****

February fourteenth arrived, and with everything packed, the three Yoshida women made their way to the bus. It would take them to the train station, where they would leave Wyoming and its winters behind at last.

Keiko found herself transported back to the first bus ride when they'd left San Francisco. It seemed a lifetime ago. This time was different, both because they were taking a new family member home, and because they were leaving another one behind.

But some things were eerily similar—the questions and uncertainty surrounding where they would live, how they would survive, and what would happen to them.

As the camp slowly disappeared behind them, still covered in snow, Keiko felt no remorse. A few of her friends had talked about missing some aspects of camp life, but Keiko, Roo, and their mother had no such misgivings. They were ready to go home, which this camp never was, and restart their lives.

Keiko had stopped by the camp post office one last time, but as with every day before, no letter from Jesse had arrived.

He'd apparently moved on. When she got back to San Francisco, she'd do the same. She wouldn't let this war tear anything more from her life.

Despite her resolve, tears found their way out, and she wiped them with her sleeve.

She forced herself to smile. "Better days are ahead."

"What?"

Keiko looked at her sister, sitting with little JT in her arms. "Nothing."

****

The next morning, Jesse sat down at the kitchen table and wrote the letter he should have written two months before. He hoped it wasn't too late.

My Dear Keiko,

I am sorry this letter is so long in coming, but the news you were still alive set my life on end. A combination of joy, confusion, and sadness took over my world as I struggled to decide the correct path for my heart.

Your letter arrived nearly three years after we last spoke, and in that time I missed you, mourned you, and went on without you. Someone new came into my life, but like you, I'd never forgotten what we had together.

The events of our lives have almost certainly changed us, probably in ways we aren't even aware of, but I have finally come to one conclusion. I still love you.

If your feelings remain the same, I look forward to hearing from you. Most of all, I wait anxiously for the day I can hold you again.

All my love, Jesse.

P.S.
Belated Happy Valentine's Day! J

Jesse re-read the letter several times, and satisfied with its content, put it in the envelope. On his way to work, he stopped at the post office, kissed the letter, and dropped it in the box.

Three weeks later, it was returned to him.

No Forwarding Address was scrawled across the front.

AUGUST, 1945

All day long, customers and friends came into the office, shaking hands and slapping backs as they celebrated the end of the war. People were relieved and filled with the anticipation of loved ones coming home from overseas. The fear of the Western Union man coming to your door with a death notice lifted like a vanishing cloud. Replacing it were anxious looks for telegrams announcing return dates.

Uncle Jerry was late getting back from lunch, and when he did show up, he carried a brown paper bag. He set it on Jesse's desk.

"Here. I thought you'd enjoy that. It's some of the best miso I've ever had."

Jesse opened the bag. "Really? Where did you get it?"

His uncle dropped down into his chair. "New place in Japantown — *Azumi's.*"

Jesse froze. "What did you say?"

"The restaurant. It's called *Azumi's.*"

"Where is it?"

"On the corner of Sutter and Laguna."

Jesse grabbed something from inside his desk, stood and headed for the door. His uncle was confused. "Aren't you going to try the miso?"

Jesse smiled.

"Yes Uncle, I most certainly am."

****

Keiko stood at the front podium sorting through the morning's receipts. With the news of the war ending, many people had been out for lunch, and the day had been busy. Since opening six weeks ago, business had built up steadily, and many of her mother's former customers had come in, glad to see the family back.

"Table for one, please."

Keiko looked up, startled by the voice. Crystalline blue eyes stared directly into hers, stealing her breath, and starting a pounding of her heart that was deafening in her ears. "Um…sure. Where would you like to sit?"

He pointed. "That booth seems to suit me perfectly."

Keiko picked up a menu, and laid it on the table directly behind her station. The man slid into the booth and handed the menu back to her. "I won't need this. Miso and water, please."

Tears welled up in her eyes. "Of course."

"Jesse!"

Keiko watched as her sister launched herself across the room. "It's so good to see you!"

She wrapped her arms around his neck, and kissed his cheek.

He gave her a big hug. "Hi, Roo. It's great to see you too. How's things?"

"Great. I'm a new momma!"

"You're kidding?"

"Nope. It's a long story, but you'll have to meet the little guy."

"I'd love to."

Roo peered at her sister, and catching Keiko's look, excused herself. "Well, I'm sure you two want to catch up. See you later, Jesse."

When Roo had retreated to the kitchen, Jesse handed Keiko an envelope.

She stared at it. "What's this?"

"I wrote that to you in February. It came back, so I wanted to deliver it myself. Read it."

Keiko settled into the seat across from Jesse and opened the letter. As she read, tears cascaded down her face, wetting the paper. She folded the letter, jumped up, and came around the table. Throwing herself onto him, she cried into his hair. "I love you, Jesse Sommers."

His own tears mingled with hers. "I love you, Keiko Yoshida."

****

The next afternoon, Jesse came into the

restaurant to pick up Keiko. Azumi was waiting for him. "It is so good to see you, Jesse."

He kissed her cheek. "And you, Mrs. Yoshida."

She struggled for words. "Jesse…"

"Yes?"

"Can you forgive us for what my husband and I did?"

Jesse smiled warmly. "It's in the past. War makes for difficult decisions."

A wide smile spread across Azumi's face. "Thank you."

Keiko came out of the back. Her long, black hair seemed to float around her deep, brown eyes, stealing his heart again, just like the first time he'd seen her.

She kissed his cheek. "Ready?"

"Yup. Let's go."

They got into his sedan and she slid across the seat next to him. A few minutes later, he parked the car in front of China Beach. They were sitting looking at the small strip of sand when Jesse took her hand. "I stopped coming here."

"When?"

"After I found out you were dead." He laughed. "At least, I *thought* you were dead."

She searched his eyes. "But you loved coming here."

He shook his head. "Not without you."

They climbed out of the car. The late

August weather was cooperating, and it was pleasant to sit on the sand, the warmth of the sun tempered by the constant breeze. Without any prompting from him, Keiko began to share the events during her time in camp.

Jesse listened intently, sensing her desire to purge herself of the pain the experience had left in her. She told him of the trip to the camp, the difficult conditions in the early days, the cold Wyoming winters, and the rape. She also shared her fond memories of the giant swimming hole, the job she did at the hospital, and the birth of Roo's baby.

She smiled broadly, thinking of the little boy. "She named him Jomei Takeshi."

"I'm sure your father was pleased."

Keiko's face clouded, her smile dissolving. He ventured a hesitant question. "How is your father?"

"He didn't come home with us."

"Oh, I'm sorry."

"It's not that he didn't want to, he couldn't."

"Why?"

She turned away from him, hiding her face. "He's in prison."

Jesse was stunned. Of all the things she might've said her father was doing, time in prison wasn't one of them. "I don't understand."

Keiko turned back, eyes red. "You remember how Roo got pregnant?"

"Sure."

"The boy responsible for the rape was killed."

"Killed?"

"Murdered."

Jesse's mouth hung open. "By your father?"

She shook her head. "No, at least I don't believe so, but he was arrested. At the trial, our lawyer said it was a 50-50 chance of father getting convicted. The judge sentenced him to thirty years."

"Oh, Keiko. I'm so sorry."

"The lawyer is appealing, but we needed to leave camp, so we came home."

He wrapped his arms around her, pulling her close to him, and kissed her. "If he's innocent, we'll get him out."

"You'd help?"

"Of course. I'd do anything for you."

She smiled up at him. "There's one thing that would make me happy forever."

"What's that?"

"As long as we live, promise you'll never let us get separated again."

He laughed. "I promise."

"Swear?"

"Swear."

A NOTE FROM THE AUTHOR

Thank you for taking the time to read my latest work. I found the research and study of the events depicted here to be a fascinating job.

Much of the content is new to me, as I was born in Canada, and did not study the events that took place in the United States during this time. As a citizen of the U.S. now, I am glad to be familiar with this chapter in our history.

While much of what went on is disturbing, I was impressed by one thing more than any other. In photograph after photograph, interview after interview, there was a smile on the face of the Japanese-Americans and little or no bitterness, despite their circumstances.

It is a resilience I won't soon forget.

For anyone interested in further study, I have included a couple links below.

Again, thank you for reading KEIKO'S WAR, and if you have any questions or comments, please let me know.

God Bless, John

COVER BY BEVERLY DALGLISH

STUDY LINKS:
http://archive.densho.org/main.aspx

http://www.heartmountain.org/index.html
http://www.digitalhistory.uh.edu/active_learning/explorations/japanese_internment/internment_timeline.cfm

****

MORE BY JOHN C. DALGLISH

THE CITY HOMICIDE SERIES

BOSTON HOMICIDE - #1
MIAMI HOMICIDE - #2
CHICAGO HOMICIDE - #3
DALLAS HOMICIDE - #4
DENVER HOMICIDE - #5

DETECTIVE JASON STRONG SERIES

WHERE'S MY SON? – #1
BLOODSTAIN – #2
FOR MY BROTHER – #3
SILENT JUSTICE – #4
TIED TO MURDER – #5
ONE OF THEIR OWN – #6
DEATH STILL - #7

LETHAL INJECTION – #8
CRUEL DECEPTION – #9
LET'S PLAY - #10
HOSTAGE - #11
CIRCLE OF FEAR - #12
DEADLY OBSESSION - #13
DEAD OF NIGHT - #14
SHADOW OF DOUBT - #15
FATAL AFFAIR - #16

THE CHASER CHRONICLES

CROSSOVER–#1
JOURNEY– #2
DESTINY-#3
INNER DEMONS-#4
DARK DAYS - #5
FAR FROM HOME - #6

Made in the USA
Monee, IL
08 March 2024